BEYOND LOVE

Middle East Literature in Translation
Michael Beard and Adnan Haydar, *Series Editors*

BEYOND LOVE

With a Foreword by miriam cooke

HADIYA HUSSEIN
Translated from the Arabic by Ikram Masmoudi

Syracuse University Press

English translation copyright © 2012 by Syracuse University Press
Syracuse, New York 13244-5290

All Rights Reserved

First Edition 2012

12   13   14   15   16   17   6   5   4   3   2   1

Originally published in Arabic as *Ma Ba'd Al-Hub* (Beirut: Arab Institution for Studies and Publication, 2004).

∞ The paper used in this publication meets the minimum requirements of the American National Standard for Information Sciences—Permanence of Paper for Printed Library Materials, ANSI Z39.48-1992.

For a listing of books published and distributed by Syracuse University Press, visit our Web site at SyracuseUniversityPress.syr.edu.

ISBN: 978-0-8156-0995-7

Library of Congress Cataloging-in-Publication Data

Husayn, Hadiyah.
    [Ma Ba'd Al-Hub. English]
    Beyond love / Hadiya Hussein ; translated from the Arabic by Ikram Masmoudi ; with a foreword by Miriam Cooke. — 1st ed.
        p. cm. — (Middle East literature in translation)
    ISBN 978-0-8156-0995-7 (pbk. : alk. paper)
    I. Masmoudi, Ikram.   II. Title.
    PJ7932.U77M313 2012
    892.7'37—dc23   2012016056

Manufactured in the United States of America

HADIYA HUSSEIN is an Iraqi writer who has published many novels and short stories. She currently lives in Amman, Jordan. *Beyond Love* is her first novel to be translated into English.

IKRAM MASMOUDI was educated in Tunisia and France, where she got her PhD from the Université Stendhal Grenoble III in textual linguistics. In 2001 she obtained the Agrégation d'arabe and taught Arabic language and culture at the Université de Provence. She has extensive teaching experience. She has taught courses of all levels of Arabic and courses on modern Arabic literature at Middlebury College, Duke University, and Princeton University. In the fall of 2008 she joined the Department of Foreign Languages and Literatures at the University of Delaware, where she chairs the Arabic Program and codirects the UD Winter Study Abroad Program in Tunisia. Her research interests are in language and literature, and she is currently working on a book about Iraqi war fiction.

CONTENTS

FOREWORD

MIRIAM COOKE

Long the capital of Arab culture, Iraq is a country that has been wracked by wars for more than a half century. However, coups, military dictatorships, the Iran-Iraq War, the Gulf War, and the American invasion have not succeeded in destroying the spirit and creativity of a people that has survived millennial violence. Women have contributed in important and distinctive ways to the construction of a vibrant and resilient culture, and Hadiya Hussein's *Beyond Love* is a noteworthy example. It is part of a genre of war literature that Arab women have been creating for the past thirty years.

The novel is set in the post-1991 period when the Shiites in southern Iraq were under surveillance and in danger of death for having participated in the uprising against Saddam Hussein shortly after the Gulf War. It tells of the price people paid for opposing the dictator or even only exercising their right not to vote for the president "who stole our lives and destroyed our hopes." Not to be a Baath member and to be generally disengaged from politics is to be under suspicion: "all citizens are guilty until they are proven innocent." The terror of the system is revealed in the assurance that "the voter's name and address are secretly printed on the voting cards. Electronic machines will find the traitors. The punishment will be stronger than they imagine." The only solution is to change identity and leave Iraq.

The novel bridges Basra/Baghdad and Amman, war and exile. Intermixing flashback, memoir, intertextual references to other Iraqi war writers, and first-person narration of exilic life in Amman, the narrator interweaves her experiences with those of Nadia, a friend who died before the novel's beginning. They are writers forced into demeaning factory work in the time of the international embargo and then into exile in Jordan after the Gulf War. They are creators whose survival challenges the destructiveness of war.

In Amman the narrator runs across Nadia's autobiographical notebook that forms a thread throughout the novel. It is a pastiche of memories strung together randomly from the story of her birth to her university years to a "hundred anxious and horrifying hours under the most violent bombing by the militaries of thirty countries" to the twenty-hour car ride to Jordan across the Iraqi desert made famous in 1963 by Ghassan Kanafani's classic story of Palestinian escape *Men in the Sun*. The narrative moves between Nadia's notebook and the narrator's deadly days in Amman.

The hardship of life in Amman is evoked through descriptions of small dirty rooms, stinking sheets, respected professionals who are lucky if they can scrape together a meager subsistence, and the enervating tedium that strips the individual of all desire to act. Dreams of home and of beautiful places far from the present hell punctuate the endless wait for work or for notification of asylum that is often refused. The depression is etched in stories of mothers who have lost contact with their sons and who are eventually sent to a place where they know nobody.

While writing about a very particular case, Hadiya Hussein takes her reader into the universal anxiety of those who have left loved ones behind, who are obsessed with the need to be in touch with them, and who are confused by the possibility of falling in love again. The fleeting promise of love for those who have been through the horrors of war and the phone that rings without answer in the far-away home vividly convey the despair of the alienated exile who no longer belongs anywhere.

ACKNOWLEDGMENTS

The translation of this novel was made possible with the help and encouragement of many friends and colleagues. I thank Hadiya Hussein for giving me the chance to translate her novel. I am also particularly indebted to miriam cooke, who gave me the idea of undertaking this translation and encouraged me throughout the process. My gratitude goes to my friend Chris Chism, who read the early draft and made helpful comments. Special thanks to my editor, Annie Barva. Finally, I thank very warmly Mary Selden Evans from Syracuse University Press for her constant encouragement.

INTRODUCTION

Hadiya Hussein is one of the leading voices in Iraqi fiction today. She has distinguished herself in the writing of short stories and novels of war and exile. *Beyond Love* is her third novel. It gives us a powerful account of the survival of the Iraqi people after senseless wars and portrays the vagrancy of those who have been forced out of the country because of war, taking us to their place of refuge: Amman, Jordan. Hussein opens her novel with a powerful verse by Lisan al-Din Ibn al-Khatib (1313–74), a famous poet and one of the greatest writers and statesmen of Muslim Spain. He was known as "the Double Vizier," a reference to his intellectual erudition and his role as a statesman. Ibn al-Khatib was accused of heresy, imprisoned in 1374, and killed by hired assassins. While in prison, he wrote powerful poetry reflecting on his destitution and his fate. Hussein chose this verse for its linguistic and stylistic subtlety:

> Great and powerful we were
> Wretched we have become;
> Yesterday we used to feast
> Today we are feasted upon.

It aptly describes the Iraqi people's situation, capturing poignantly how, once forming a great nation, they became subjugated and fell into a state of decrepitude and ruin under the dictatorship of Saddam Hussein and the many wars he brought upon the country.

An Iraqi exile in Amman since the 1990s, Hussein narrates in *Beyond Love* the loss and perdition that befell her country after the First Gulf War in 1991. During the thirteen years of economic sanctions that followed the war, the people suffered not only the scarcity of food and necessary products, but the lack of freedom and a strangling state of surveillance and fear from constantly tightening government control. Many of the Iraqis who could afford to do so fled the country—some left under false identities, others under medical excuses. Long before the current war and its dramatic consequences on the fabric of Iraqi society, Iraqis had already become a scattered people, revealing their pain throughout the world and reopening their wounds in an effort to come to terms with the past and heal their memory. Despite its lack of opportunities, Amman is the closest border for the fugitive Iraqi people and a meeting point where they tell their sorrow and grief while waiting to be granted refugee status or to be relocated somewhere else in the world through the Office of the United Nations High Commissioner for Refugees.

One of the most illuminating aspects of the novel is its narration of the defeat of 1991, the Shiite uprising in Basra and southern Iraq, and the impact of the years of sanctions. Basra and southern Iraq are very important in the novel. Two of the main characters, Nadia and Moosa, originated there, and both give us firsthand accounts about what happened. Basra is one of the most important towns in Iraq. Its religious ties with and geographic proximity to Iran and its closeness to Kuwait are important factors in any attempt to understand how the people of this town and of southern Iraq in general were impacted and their lives stigmatized by successive wars with Iran and then with Kuwait and the coalition forces led by the United States in the First Gulf War. Basra's population is mostly Shiite, and many collectively felt marginalized and excluded from genuine participation and collaboration with the northern Sunni communities during Saddam Hussein's regime. It was from Basra that Iraqi troops went south to invade Kuwait in August 1990, and it was to Basra that they returned defeated in February 1991. The novel poetically documents the Iraqi army's humiliation through Moosa, a soldier returning from Kuwait to Basra. He describes how these beaten soldiers not only had to swallow their bitterness and mortification, but also were targeted and crushed by air attacks as they went home.

This defeat triggered a large-scale uprising of the southern Shiite community. The spark started in Basra and spread to other southern towns. The South in general had suffered much devastation during the Iran-Iraq War and the Gulf War and had provided the army with the bulk of its infantry units. In addition to citizens and demoralized troops who returned from the front, the revolt involved support from agents of the Islamic Dawa Party and some Iraqi Shia militant groups based in Iran. According to Anthony Cordesman and Ahmed Hashim, "The uprising began when infantry soldiers streamed back to Basra bringing back with them tales of horror and defeat. These troops and sympathetic Shi'ites citizens launched attacks against government installations, including security party and popular army buildings. . . . [W]ithin days the revolt had spread to major cities including the holy cities of Karbala and Najaf as well as the towns of Diwaniya, al-Hillah, al-Kut and al-Amarah and Mahmoudiya."[1]

The Shiite revolt spread and benefited from the presence of the coalition forces and from the help of Iraqi militant groups who were based in Iran. But the uprising failed to take root because of a lack of organization and the absence of a clear vision. The Iraqi Republican Guard eventually brutally crushed it; within a few weeks, thousands of people were killed, and many more died during the following months. In addition, nearly two million people fled for their lives. Cordesman and Hashim describe the aftermath: "The rebels paid a heavy price when the Iraqi government fought back with its most loyal units, the Republican Guards, and made liberal use of helicopter gunships in the towns where the rebels were holed up. A large number of hapless civilians caught up in the crossfire fled into the zone of the Marshes, the coalition controlled areas, or even into Iran. The tide turned in the government's favor when Basra and Karbala were secured on March 12 and 17, 1991."[2]

The regime put to death captured rebels or tortured them in the most horrifying ways. In the novel, the character Nadia fled with her family from Basra to Baghdad when the uprising was crushed. In her diary, she relates how all those who escaped the violence in the South had to be relocated in Basra in 1993. Her lover was among the soldiers who disappeared during the uprising and never returned. Through her diary and her letters to him from

1. Anthony H. Cordesman and Ahmed S. Hashim, *Iraq: Sanctions and Beyond* (Boulder, Colo.: Westview Press, 1997), 101.

2. Ibid., 102.

her exile in Amman, her love comes across stronger than all the machinery of war and the years of exile that separate her from him.

The novel's historical context is also dominated by the consequences of the strict economic sanctions imposed by the United Nations against Iraq. Because of the sanctions, Iraq's population was devastated socially, economically, and psychologically. The novel's female characters, Nadia and Huda, experience deprivation and disempowerment in Baghdad while they work at the al-Amal Factory (Factory of Hope) for men's underwear. An unhealthy atmosphere of fear and humiliation dominates the factory, and the women workers are abused and controlled by a ruthless boss paradoxically named "Shafiqa," the Arabic word for "kindness" and "sympathy." The atmosphere in the factory replicates the feeling of the whole country. The women working in these humiliating conditions are widows, divorcées, and young women unable to find husbands. They try to survive in a country where the living conditions have become very difficult in the absence of men, who would under normal circumstances be providing for them. Stubbornness pushes Huda, the main character and one of the workers in the factory, to write "No" instead of the required "Yes" on her ballot in a presidential election. But fear of the consequences of her action compels her to flee the country to Amman, leaving behind her grandmother and the Baghdad she loves to join the lines of Iraqis who wait in front of the Refugee Office.

Her life in Amman is full of sad encounters, grief, and remembrance. In the form of letters, diaries, and memoirs of the war, the defeat, and the uprising, Hussein's characters—Huda, her coworker Nadia, and Moosa, whom Huda meets at the Refugee Office in Amman— give their accounts of these years of fear and torture.

BEYOND LOVE

Great and powerful we were
Wretched we have become;
Yesterday we used to feast
Today we are feasted upon.
—Lisan al-Din Ibn al-Khatib,
the Double Vizier (1313–74)

"This is everything."

A leather handbag containing a wallet with many pockets and a small notebook . . . a pair of jeans, a long coat, four woolen sweaters, three shirts . . . a few books—some literary and some about Iraq during and after Desert Storm—and a large notebook for memories . . . a ceramic cup containing seashells, colored beads, and small, strangely shaped stones—I had no idea where Nadia had gotten them. "I'll keep just the books and the handbag," I told the landlady before losing myself again in the street. "You can give the rest to those who might need it." Nadia's death had struck me like a thunderbolt. How, I wondered, can a car driven by a reckless driver end the life of someone looking only for a safe refuge after fleeing the hell of her homeland?

The street swallowed me. It was as tumultuous with the noise of cars and pedestrians as my mind was with its many questions and a single, unwavering answer: "This is how death comes, as a visitor whose knock you never expect at your door. Sometimes it enters without knocking and surprises you before you stand up. Death has the keys to everything locked and doesn't need permission to enter."

I mourned her silently and painfully in my tiny refuge, a room high on the slopes of Mount al-Hussein and cursed the day I'd run into her again. Our memories were supposedly buried in Baghdad. What made them come back to the surface again, weaving once more their web of sorrow and exile in Amman?

OUR ENCOUNTER in Amman was unexpected; in fact, it seemed impossible. Even when I was still in Baghdad, I never thought we would meet again; I always thought she had settled in Basra. The last time I called her was in 1994, just before all the phone numbers were changed. Over those years, memory had finally come to the verge of throwing off the weight it carried. How else could it handle all the calamities, the wars, the embargo, the uprooting? In the Friday market near the Abdali complex, crowded with people, cars, vintage clothing, peddlers, beggars, vegetable merchants, and food kiosks, there we were, side by side. Fate had squeezed us into a narrow corner between a wall of used clothes suspended like hanging corpses and piles of garments crammed into closed boxes and smelling of mothballs. At first, I didn't notice our chance proximity. We were turning over the clothes, looking for the ones that were clean and cheap.

We might have gone our separate ways if it hadn't been for her voice, full of Iraqi grief. "What's the problem? Everything is so expensive. You have to bring the price down."

I started, snatching my hands back from the shirt I was about to buy.

When I first heard her voice, I wasn't sure that it was Nadia. I don't know if I was attracted by the language—I missed speaking with an Iraqi accent—or if my subconscious recognized her first.

There we were, face-to-face after a handful of years—mute, paralyzed. We could find nothing to say. It was as if each of us wanted to release a cry from the depths, but the cry withdrew, clearing the way for tears. We didn't know whether the source of our tears was the joy of the encounter or the sadness about what we had left behind. We stared at each other a long moment before we broke out with names . . . and tears.

THE STORY of my first encounter with Nadia starts at a men's underwear factory called Factory of Hope, Factory of Amal, located at al-Karrada and owned by Mr. Fatih. He was a corpulent man with a dark complexion, prominent belly, and bald head hidden by a cotton hat. He usually came into the factory after two o'clock and never stayed more than two hours. He confidently left arrangements and regulations to the watchful supervision of Shafiqa, a woman heading toward her forties with a constantly terrified but alert face.

Shafiqa had a sharp and fiery temperament. She had earned her authority through her fierce commitment to handling everything, big or small, as though she were the real owner of the factory. When she spoke, she waved her hands to the left and to the right as if shooting the words from between her fingers. As soon as she finished speaking, she would drop her hands down by her sides, where they looked forlorn without any movement. Her kohl-lined eyes constantly roamed the corners of the rectangular room, where she controlled twenty-five female workers sitting behind sewing machines for eight hours a day. The humid room had only one window, which looked out on a small yard used for the lunch break, and was decorated with shoddy handwritten excerpts from the speeches of the president, whose portrait hung at the factory entrance.

One day, two months after I'd started working at the factory, Shafiqa walked in. A svelte, brown-skinned young woman with thick black hair hanging to her shoulders accompanied her. Shafiqa introduced her as Nadia Mazloom, pointed to a place for her right behind me, and gave her a scarf to tie her hair. After a single look from Shafiqa, we returned to work as though we hadn't heard anything. The machines' clamor rose again.

During the first few days, Nadia seemed withdrawn. She allowed others into her world only to a certain point; when asked about anything, she would reply only briefly. She used to sit away from the others during the break, and after she heard the bell, she would hurry back to her machine as though escaping us. The women disapproved of her behavior and thought she was full of herself.

To me, she seemed like an incomprehensible book. But I nevertheless became the person closest to her. After some time, I felt that she was like a banana skin: with a little bit of patience, it was possible to unpeel it and find the sweet and soft fruit inside. I also noticed her distraction when she spoke or was spoken to; she would suddenly fall silent, seemingly unable to utter anything, as if she were sick. But this would last only a few seconds. Salwa once accused Nadia of being disrespectful because she didn't listen to whoever was speaking and of cutting that person off.

After our relationship grew stronger, I asked Nadia about her strange state of distraction. She informed me that she had suffered from it for almost three years and didn't know what she was thinking of when it happened. It was like a deep sleep empty of any dreams. I used to tell her that it was a blessing because we get distracted only when we are pressured and exhausted from the troubles of life. If these troubles remain hard to forget, the pain will expand into the very depths of our souls. Sometimes she would respond with an obscure smile, and sometimes she looked unconcerned.

One time when we were sitting in a corner away from the others, her eyes blurred, and she looked absentminded. I shook her shoulders, saying, "Hey, I'm jealous of the man you are thinking about."

She smiled unambiguously. She said, "I'm looking for something precious I lost. Sometimes, unexpectedly, it comes to me, but before I take hold of it, it departs and vanishes."

I pushed her gently. "Who is he?"

She lowered her head, saying, "I will cry if I say anything. Let's leave this for another time."

I didn't ask her about it again after that, and the opportunity didn't come until many years later. By then, Nadia had been killed, but she had left the answer in a handful of letters.

DAY BY DAY the closed book opened to me. I quietly read pages that revealed a dreaming, gentle-hearted person. She and I were calmly weaving the lengthening threads of our friendship. We met each other outside work and exchanged a few visits. I learned that she was a graduate of the College of Administration and Economics in Basra. She had tried her hand at writing short stories, but she never showed them to anyone. Perhaps this was the strongest thread that bound our friendship. I, too, used to enjoy literature and had tried my hand at poetry. I even dared publish a poem, then followed that one with a second and a third. I had graduated with a degree in Arabic language and literature and still read literature and enjoyed the arts. Yet, for some reason, I gave up poetry. Perhaps poetry was no longer able to convey our sorrows.

I thought of asking her about that lost thing she missed in her life but always deferred doing so. Maybe I wanted her to confess it voluntarily so that I wouldn't seem curious or meddlesome about her affairs.

THERE WAS NO HOPE in the Factory of Hope. Just a group of women looking for daily bread dipped in misery after the loss of opportunities, the lengthy siege, and the destruction of the country: pseudowomen sitting behind deaf machines that devoured their lives and shrank their faces. Some of them were illiterate—widows, divorcées, spinsters. Others were married in name only, preferring the protection of any man just so they weren't considered divorced. Some were young girls whose dreams were bigger than their reality.

The powerful, vicious Shafiqa supervised us, acting on behalf of a man who knew less about his factory than she did. Aziza and Salwa received the biggest share of rebuke and reprimand from Shafiqa, for they were the only quarrelsome ones.

Aziza was an active and shapely twenty-five-year-old with prominent breasts whose nipples could not be hidden by summer shirts. Her mouth was sensual, her gaze dreamy. She was always in a good mood, and her

cheeks were naturally so rosy that one day Shafiqa shook
her finger at her in warning, saying, "This is a factory, not
a nightclub! Makeup is forbidden! Remove that red color
from your cheeks."

Aziza took one of the flannels right away and rubbed
her cheeks with it. She spread it before Shafiqa's eyes and
then displayed it for everyone to see. "Look," she said. "It
is white like snow. God alone has put this makeup on my
face from the day I was born."

When Shafiqa left the room, Aziza burst out, "Oh,
God, when will you save me? Let me marry a man, no
matter how he looks, as long as he rescues me from hardship and this cursed country, the country of endless
wars!" Then she returned to work, and after a few minutes her good humor settled back in.

Aziza never lost an opportunity to say something
crude. When she finished sewing a piece, she would hold
it up and say, "I wonder who the guy is who will hide
his privates behind this." No one shared her jokes except
Salwa. We couldn't hear them, but their meaning was
obvious. Their eyes brimmed with tears of laughter suppressed out of fear of Shafiqa.

Salwa's face showed contrasting expressions. Sometimes she would look innocent, and sometimes the
secrets of a well-experienced woman seemed to be hiding behind her honey-colored eyes. She was agile, talk-
ative, and quarrelsome. For unknown reasons, she had
declared herself an enemy of Mother Khadija, although
the latter was in her sixties and this job was her only
source of pleasure. Despite the wrinkles, traces of beauty
were still apparent beneath the sadness on Mother Khadija's face.

In stark contrast to all of these women, though, was Nadia. She was mostly silent, and everything about her was uncommon—her figure, her clothing, her behavior. Her eyes lured us with a mysterious attraction, but I wasn't sure whether we were drawn because of her eyes or the tone of her calm voice or the way she spoke when she suddenly became vacant and appeared like a woman from a bygone age. She didn't take part in discussions and didn't argue, so she was the only one of us who was spared Shafiqa's tongue, from which even I couldn't preserve myself in spite of my great caution.

One morning when it was raining and the streets were muddy, I had trouble getting to the factory. Just before I sat behind my machine, Shafiqa's authoritarian voice assaulted me, making it clear to everyone that she would not permit this breach of discipline. When I told her that being five minutes late should be understandable on such a rainy day, she mocked me. She started counting the damage it would cause to Mr. Fatih, our benefactor, if it were to happen again. Then she sneered at the graduate student who ignored the importance of time and didn't understand the slogan written with sparkling letters and hanging over our heads. She pointed with her fingers and spat the words, "To lose a minute of work is to lose an opportunity for progress." It was hard to remain impassive in front of Shafiqa, but I hid the irony I felt regarding a slogan often repeated by a president who was in fact the one who stole our lives and destroyed our hopes.

After Shafiqa rebuked me on that cold morning, she announced menacingly that because of the recession, Mr. Fatih had decided to do without a certain number of workers. She said she was going to post a list of the workers who exceeded the factory's need. Obviously, she used this announcement to make us nervous. It would be logical for Shafiqa to choose the less productive or the undisciplined workers, but Salwa pointed out another reason that she believed would be the main one used for dismissal.

Shafiqa walked out after making the announcement, leaving us helpless and scared. We were anxious and wanted to know what was going on. Salwa stood up at this moment, though, and malignantly announced that Shafiqa would choose those who might be her rivals for Mr. Fatih's heart. After Salwa dropped this bomb, she refused to give more details until the break bell rang. Aziza immediately asked her what she meant, but Salwa, fearing that Shafiqa might hear, whispered words that we couldn't hear. Still, the other women wouldn't let Salwa possess the secret alone. They threw themselves around her so that she couldn't escape their curiosity.

"You don't need to be smart to figure it out. Mr. Fatih has lived alone since his Syrian wife left him a few days before the war broke out. Since then, she hasn't come back, perhaps because he is getting fat and she's afraid she won't be able to breathe under him. Isn't this a good reason for Shafiqa to hope that she might marry that heap of flesh? Having already missed the boat, she is jealous and tightening her control over us so that no one will get the chance to have him for herself."

Aziza laughed coquettishly, saying, "Just one glance from me would be enough to drag him to bed, but I don't want to die suffocated."

Quick glances circulated, and the low laughter was stifled out of fear that Shafiqa would crush the merriment. Mother Khadija found herself squeezed between

Salwa and Aziza, buffeted by their words until she pulled herself away from them, begging God's forgiveness and throwing Salwa a glance of recrimination.

Salwa went on, reminding us how difficult it was even to approach Mr. Fatih, for it was necessary to go through Shafiqa first if we needed to talk to him. Shafiqa would enter the room with us for anything of a truly serious nature.

At this point, Mother Khadija asked the others to stop their nonsense, which might threaten our only source of income. She looked at Salwa severely. Salwa became so angry that she damned the day Mother Khadija entered the factory, forgetting that the older woman had already been there when Salwa herself had started working.

Things would have stopped there had not Aziza winked at Salwa, saying, "Male underwear seems to have its effect."

Before the laughter had completely died down, Salwa glared at Mother Khadija and yelled, "If you don't like this conversation, don't push yourself into it! You are an elderly woman, and it is not suitable for you, so don't interfere!"

All the while, Nadia and I had been observing, not participating. After a short time, Nadia chose to move to the corner farthest away, and Mother Khadija withdrew from Salwa and Aziza, hissing to Salwa, "You are the last person to talk about people's honor!"

Salwa became even angrier, and all the women held their breath out of fear of an unexpected explosion, as sometimes happened. But Aziza took hold of Salwa and moved her away from Mother Khadija. All we could hear then were muttered insults.

Mother Khadija and Salwa had never liked each other and never agreed on anything. The clash between them, however, would go only so far. There was a certain point beyond which neither was willing to step. Years later the hidden nuances of their relationship were disclosed to me when I encountered Mother Khadija once again in Amman. Both she and Salwa had originated from al-Shawaka, a forgotten quarter in Baghdad, with cracked houses and overflowing sewers in wintertime. Even today the houses' walls are half washed away by humidity during the rainy season, and termites build nests in their pillars and wooden roofs. Bogs and ponds find their way to its alleys, which sink below street level during the rainy season. It is a quarter falling into oblivion for everyone but the rats, the scorpions, and poverty.

After the break, all the women returned to their machines except Salwa, who stood again in the front part of the room. Looking upset, she announced, "If Shafiqa dismisses me, I will dishonor her."

Mumbles and questions circulated in the room. Aziza exploded in support, but the other women asked what Salwa meant.

Feeling she had said enough, Salwa simply returned to her place, adding, "All of you are self-serving. You'll compete in flattering Shafiqa so that she spares you. Don't rush things; I for one will wait for the list, and then we'll see what happens."

The machines' rising clamor interfered with our questions and laughter, drowning out everything but Shafiqa's sharp command to get back to work. At four o'clock we brushed off our hands and ran to the coat rack.

A WEEK LATER Mr. Fatih fired five women. None of them made any objection, for there was no law to protect employees in the private factories. Contrary to our expectations, Salwa was not among the fired women. One month later, however, she announced that she was leaving to marry someone who was employed at the Ministry of Commerce. Mother Khadija was one of the first to congratulate her; she took Salwa in her arms and wished her a happy life.

Aziza lowered her eyes and embarked on a long daydream before saying to Salwa, "You are the first; we are next."

At that time, the market was in its worst economic recession, although underwear wasn't as greatly affected as other merchandise. Nevertheless, Mr. Fatih reduced the number of workers again. Shafiqa informed us of the cuts, but the news didn't have the same impact on us as it had the first time. The whole country was in turmoil; major atrocities were broadcast by the channel of the president's son. They were crimes reminiscent of the days of Abu Tabar in the 1970s before we found out that Abu Tabar, who robbed people's tranquillity and security, was nothing more than a creature of the regime.[1]

A FEW WORDS, fragments of jokes, complaints, and vexations—this was our life in the Factory of Hope. Over time, we had become weaker parts of the machines. Sometimes we forced a laugh, but it vanished immediately, or we voiced our complaints but never received a response.

---

1. Abu Tabar, the "Father of the Ax," a supposed serial killer who terrorized Baghdad in 1972–73, but who was in fact working for Saddam Hussein's regime, killing those families who opposed it.

The floating flannel particles clung to our clothes and our eyelashes, dulling the shine in our eyes. And whenever Shafiqa wanted to punish one of us, she would assign that woman to the storage room to find the damaged pieces and repair what could be repaired.

The storage room was just seven by five feet, with no other opening than the door. The ventilation was very bad, the light scarce, and the humidity suffocating. We used to call it the "prison cell." Shafiqa, who had much experience in the market, never missed an opportunity to benefit from small pieces of fabric. She asked us to collect these pieces in bags after the selection process. Then she would sell them to the Dushma factories on her own initiative, not Mr. Fatih's, because he never thought about taking such measures. The system was lifeless, rigorous, numbing.

On the days the machine technician visited the factory, the lonely souls were stirred and the usual order was shaken. Emad was a tall young man with a clear complexion and an elegant appearance. He used to come every Saturday to examine and repair the damaged machines because under the endless embargo Mr. Fatih couldn't import new ones. Emad also came on other occasions, for an hour or two when necessary.

Every Saturday the women prettied themselves as though they were going to a party; they would wear lipstick and sparkling eye shadow. As soon as they saw the handsome technician, their faces drained of color and their eyes attacked him with improper looks. Aziza would claim that her machine was too heavy, and Salwa would complain about the quality of the needles that pulled at and damaged the fabric. A third woman would ask him, although she knew the answer already, whether Mr. Fatih would buy new machines. Another woman would call out: "Please, Mr. Emad, have a look at my machine! It's getting tired." No matter how long he stayed, they always had questions and requests the entire time. He spent his visit observing the machines, taking notes, recording requests, and promising every woman that he would take care of her demand. Infatuated eyes and lascivious glances would always follow him as he departed.

Shafiqa often noticed those eyes and glances, though. She realized that unless she set things straight, she would lose control of the situation. One day she said to Mr. Fatih, "How can you set a fire near gasoline?" So one Saturday another engineer stepped in. He was short and pushing toward his sixties, with only a little white hair left on his scalp. And so Emad appeared and quickly disappeared, like a dream, as Aziza kept saying. Still, he wasn't a dream because we had a collective feeling about him. But so it was that the status quo was reasserted.

WE SANK TO THE PAVEMENT, devastated, our fingers intertwined while silently we wept.

"How long have you been here?" I asked her.

She replied with a dry voice, as if it came from the heart of the desert. "A year and a half. Only a few days more, though, before I move to Canada. I live very poorly on a small wage from the Refugee Office and what I earn at the boutique selling children's clothes. And you?"

"I just arrived. I applied for asylum, and I'm still waiting for the interview."

We sank into silence again. We looked at each other as if trying to discover our inmost secrets or as if looking for things lost: the remaining traces of our humanity crushed under the wheels of chaos.

She finally broke the silence, seeming to talk to herself. "Will anyone believe what happened to us? The children of a wealthy country scattered all over the world?"

I didn't answer. The sidewalk couldn't absorb the overflow of our emotions, so I suggested that we go to my "house," meaning my room, which was perched on top of a carpentry workshop on Mount al-Hussein. On our way, we held hands and exchanged glances, not believing in this meeting.

I prepared tea. She wanted Iraqi tea.

"Don't put any sage or mint in it."

"As you like."

While we were drinking tea, I looked at her face carefully. It had lost its shining light. I also noticed her weakened body. I couldn't help asking, "What happened after we went our separate ways?"

She stared at me, the shadow of a pale smile flowing into her eyes, so I felt it was inappropriate to ask her about her circumstances. I wanted to rephrase my question to fill the gap that had opened between us, but she went on, as if she realized that in exile we had nothing but words to express our tragedy.

"You know the ruin that befell the country soon after you left it. But if you are asking specifically about me, I have lost everything. They killed my brother, Nadir. My mother died of grief and sadness just two months after him. And the man I loved disappeared somewhere in this world."

Words froze on my lips for a few seconds. Nadir had been a strong man, with light-brown skin, wide eyes, a light mustache, and curly hair. When I first visited Nadia's family, he had been standing at the door. I'd smiled at him as though I'd known him for many years and said, "You are Nadir. Nadia has told me about you."

He'd said jokingly, "And how do you find me? Do I really look like Alessandro?"[2]

I'd said confidently, "Of course not. You are better looking. You have Sumerian features."

Nadia looked into the distance, reminding me of those days at the Factory of Hope when she used to roam far away. Then she said intensely, "Death flourishes in our country. It has become like any growing trade and has found supporters and allies possessing the ugliest technologies of torture."

She put down her cup with some tea still in it. Without allowing me to comment, she continued. "One of the traders washed his hands of his own crime and instead pushed Nadir into hell. Nadir was unemployed after he finished his military service—you know how it is. He used to spend most of his time in the coffeehouse or praying in the mosque with his friends. After the police raids started targeting the mosques, he listened to my mother when she begged him, 'My son, God alone will protect you from their evil. He knows the secrets of all things. You can pray at home; you don't need collective prayer in these circumstances.' Then after a while Nadir worked as a truck driver with Hamid Kalla, one of the merchants of Shourja Market."

She leaned against the wall, tears suspended behind her eyelids. "Nadir didn't know what fate had in store.

2. Alessandro: a character in a famous Mexican film series.

Between the cartons of merchandise, Hamid was smuggling banned packs of foreign cigarettes. At that time, as you know, the country was not stable. People were escaping military service and the militia's forced training; there were conspiracies and feuds among the speculators to dominate some or all of the market of smuggled oil. There were suspicious brokers and middlemen, pamphlets posted on walls everywhere, and weapons and students could cross the borders for the right price. Nadir was stopped at the checkpoint between Baghdad and Basra and the contraband cigarettes were discovered.

"Nadir was condemned to fifteen years in prison for committing an economic crime during a state of emergency. We didn't know if this incident was part of a conspiracy to get rid of the youth who were attending mosques or if Hamid was just a cigarette smuggler who in order to protect himself denied any involvement in the crime when it was discovered."

She swallowed as if parched. I gave her some water and suggested that she rest, but she continued. "The last thing my mother said on her deathbed—she had become a heap of ashes inside her clothes—was, 'If only my belly had kept having miscarriages and had dried out and decayed.'"

Nadia was overcome by distraction. After a moment, she emerged from her thoughts and asked, "How is it possible to die like this? The world is moved by the death of a child here or there but is deaf and blind to our gratuitous deaths."

She looked at me. "Do you know, Huda, what hurts us in being away from our country is not just the exile, but our bleeding memory. Even though that memory was once beautiful, it digs deeply now and reshapes the past like an enemy laying an ambush. The few happy moments that we witnessed have buried themselves in deep domes within our memory, and we can't find them without suffering still more wounds—as though we're eager to torture ourselves and whip our souls for reasons we don't understand. Tragedy wears us like clothing."

I asked her how the prison penalty became a death penalty.

She was absorbed; thousands of sharp blades seemed to pierce her heart, and her eyes remained full of tears. She looked away. "Once a month my mother and I used to visit him in prison. At every visit, his body was thinner, but his determination to take revenge on Hamid Kalla remained strong. We tried to find a way to calm his excitement, but in vain; it was like looking for a needle on a floor filled with straw. His eyes lost their sparkle, and the veins of his hands stood out as if he'd aged twenty years. Meanwhile, the president forgot all about issuing any pardon for the prisoners."

I said to her, "He has no time. He is always busy planning wars."

She sighed and said, "Ah, Huda, every time I want to get away from these tragedies, I get drawn back to them. The past that we buried has left us with no present through which to reach another life. The irony is that we all recount the same stories even though we know that every Iraqi has been burned by this fire."

I poured some more tea, saying, "These stories are all that we have. We ought to repeat them again and again in order to bear witness to the age of butcheries.

You have to speak, Nadia. Tell me why they put Nadir to death."

A cloud passed over her eyes, and she looked absent-minded, as if her soul had been pulled out of her body. Then she seemed to wake up suddenly, as if from an oppressive nightmare. "Although the political prisoners were put into individual cells, they were able to reach other prisoners and to organize a cell that was called the Delivery Cell. It was a small cell in the beginning, but it grew bigger because the prisoners' pain brought them to the brink. Then one day, in the last shadows of the night, they exploded. The truth is some of the guards helped them—otherwise, the guns would not have made their way to them—and after dawn prayer call the prison was in flames. The prisoners almost prevailed, but four and a half hours were enough for the regime to send in the necessary support to regain control of the prison. Some fled, some were killed, and the rest were put to death without trial. Nadir was among those who had joined the Delivery Cell."

I mourned with her, but I pulled myself together sharply and said with regret, "We must have committed major errors in order to arrive at so wrong a place. I sometimes despair because I see that our weak silence about those big wrongs is what stole our confidence and held us back. The consequence was that we assumed unconsciously the guilt both for those crimes and for not fighting them."

Nadia didn't comment; my words echoed in my ears, and I was struck by the triviality of what I'd said. I abruptly broke into convulsive laughter. She put her hand on my forehead and said, "Laugh, Huda. Some laughter is like tears."

We fell silent for a little while as we tried to escape the painful memories. Then she asked, "When is your interview with the Refugee Office?"

"I don't know. I don't even know about the format of the interview."

"They will ask for the circumstances of your flight from Iraq and the possibility of your return. You have to answer carefully because if you have any chance of returning, they will cross your name out."

"Oh, Nadia, how can I return after what I did?"

"What did you do?"

The long, painful memories of my journey descended upon me, and I said, "I fled because of a foolish thing I should not have done."

I started telling her about that unfortunate day when they made us crawl to the polls to write just one word, "Yes." We were to write it in support of a president who had no rival. Because I wanted to overcome the fear that was rooted in me, I decided to say "No," despite all the warnings from my cousin Youssef. When I told him my idea, he assured me that even if the entire people said "No," the result would indisputably be "Yes." Nevertheless, I was stubborn, and I wrote "No."

My neighbor was responsible for the party's masquerades in our quarter.[3] Although my neighbor and I had never openly clashed, our relationship was unfriendly.

---

3. "The party": the Baath Party, which was the only party of government in Iraq until 2003.

She was unable to drag me into the party, and I hated the regime that brought wars and woes upon the country. I used to avoid her and strove to bite my tongue whenever I met her in the street. On celebration days, I used to leave home so that she couldn't oblige me to participate. I would take my grandmother to my aunt Umm Youssef's place in Kadhimiya until the clamor of the celebrations calmed down.[4]

The most important thing is that I said "No." I wrote it stubbornly, as though extinguishing the dictator's last breath. Then I left the polling center, which was decorated with portraits of him. The numerous poor were strung out in long lines. Some of them were shouting with joy, thinking they were going to get an increase in rations, as had been promised them. When I came back home, I felt better and more energetic than I ever had before, so much so that I didn't complain about my grandmother's many requests on that day. Rather, I put my head next to her hands, asking her to caress my hair as she used to do when I was a child.

The following morning someone knocked on the door. I found myself standing toe-to-toe with my neighbor, looking at her sad, inflexible face that usually never knew smiles. On this occasion, though, she displayed a big smile that ill-suited her sharp features. She asked to come in. I showed her a deference she didn't deserve, despite already knowing why she was there. Feigning nonchalance, I asked her if she preferred tea or coffee, but she refused and immediately said, "I have no time. I'm

---

4. *Umm:* the Arabic word for "mother."

tired. We sorted out the votes until late yesterday, and we found five ballots from our region with the word 'No.'"

I said unconcernedly, "I wonder who are the stupid ones who would dare to do such a thing?"

She looked at me with a glance both wily and threatening and said, "It will not be difficult for us to find out—the voter's name and address are secretly printed on the voting cards. Electronic machines will find the traitors. The punishment will be stronger than they imagine."

I don't know how I contained myself enough to reply, "Human life cannot be determined by machines; they might be wrong."

Her cunning glance penetrated me. She spoke with a deep desire to torture me. "Although the machines cannot be wrong because they are imported from a highly developed country, experts in handwriting will also go over the names."

She was belching between her sentences and frightening me more and more. She asked, "Are you one of them?"

My heart sank, but I controlled my emotions. Holding tenaciously to my calm, I said, "What would push me to do such a scandalous thing?" I was avoiding her questions with other questions that pulled the danger away from me, if only for an instant.

She replied, staring at me, "Because you stubbornly refuse to join the party and don't participate in any patriotic activity. For us, these things demonstrate a negative attitude."

I smiled faintly. "That's not enough to accuse me. Is it possible that the one who did it is a member of the party in name only?" Not giving her the opportunity to respond, I continued questioning her. "Didn't the president say that all Iraqis are Baathist even if they are not affiliated?"

"But, for us, all citizens are guilty until they are proven innocent."

"Of what are they accused?"

"Disloyalty to the leader and therefore failure to contribute to the march of the revolution."

"Who distinguishes loyalty from disloyalty?"

"We, the protectors of the principles, we do."

I was furious, but I held back, saying, "So if there are secret ink and experts in handwriting, why do you waste your time with me?"

She looked at me with narrowed eyes and said, "Listen, before it is too late, confess to me, and I will see what I can do. You are a woman like me, and we are neighbors. That is the only way—after this, things will be out of my hands."

I said with the same faint smile on my face, "I have nothing else to discuss."

Her face was flushed. "I assert that what you declare here is not the truth. You have had a chance that might not be offered again. I fear an ill-fated end for you." She belched again and left.

One hour later I woke up my grandmother, gathered her belongings, and told her that I had seen my mother in a dream, so I had to go to Najaf to visit her tomb. I told my grandmother she had to stay with my aunt until my return. I had believed the story about the handwriting experts and the secret ink and fearfully started making up scenarios about what was going to happen to me.

Only Youssef knew about my fears. He was angry and kept asking, "What did you do to yourself? Didn't I warn you?" That very day he took me to his friend's house, and before twenty-four hours had passed, he had arranged a passport with a false identity for me. This was how I fled, leaving behind my belongings, my grandmother, and the beautiful memory of my past.

I STACKED NADIA'S BOOKS on a small table, hung up the handbag, and picked up the notebook. On the first page was some poetry by George Saidah. It was written with big letters as if it were the title for what followed:

How can you leave?
How can I not go with you?

I started reading what Nadia had written on the next page:

I thank exile, for it gives me time to reorganize my papers and catch the fleeting details. I reshape them and blow the spirit into them, and here I'm starting from those forgotten days, from that womb that used to have miscarriages.

On a long night, in a cold month in 1963, during a winter with endless rain that steeped the wretched houses, Juri was in labor. This was just one day after the lifting of the curfew after the coup d'état of February 8.

Outside the muddy house in that nameless village, the wind was howling, and the thunder muffled the cries of the woman in labor while Mazloom al-Sa'idi sat with shaking fingers and dry lips, smoking a rolled cigarette. Between him and Juri there was a dying fireplace where, from time to time throughout the unbearably long night, he stirred the burning coals to life. His cigarette fell when Juri let out a cry that made him think the baby had finally slipped out.

But the baby hadn't slipped out. Juri kept moaning and gripping the bed with her fingers, while Mazloom al-Sa'idi tried to comfort her, hoping for the morning.

She gnashed her teeth, calling, "I can't! You have to do something lest I die!"

The thunderstorm didn't stop. Darkness reigned heavily over the houses, the lamp hanging from the low roof of the room shaking, its light flickering.

Mazloom put on his woolen coat, rolled his *koufiya* around his head, and courageously waded through the flooded streets. The wind's sounds brought desolation to his heart, and the shaking branches produced strange voices like the muttering of devils.

It was one hour after midnight, and the darkness hid the street's features. The houses' closed doors were clothed in deep shadow. Mazloom held fast to the wet fences, and the lightning showed him where to put his feet. He entered a narrow, twisted alley and then arrived at the door of the midwife, Lami'a's door. He knocked a few times, and the echo faded in the night. He continued knocking with cold, rigid hands until he heard a rough voice asking him, "Who's there?"

"I'm Mazloom al-Sa'idi. My wife is in labor."

"Oh, man, you are terrible. How can you come at this time of night?"

"People don't choose the instant of their birth—you know this."

"But my joints won't help me. Can you wait until morning?"

"It's not in my hands. If she could wait, I wouldn't have come."

"It must be a girl; their delivery is hard, and their lives are even worse."

He was deeply anxious while he held the hand of the fat midwife, who carried her leather tool bag in her other hand. He thought that perhaps God was punishing him for some offense he must have committed. Otherwise, why was his wife giving birth to a fourth female child? Although all these infants had died just a few days after their births, Mazloom al-Sa'idi was shattered every time his wife lost her baby, feeling responsible for its death because of his constant prayers to God to give him a male child. He would remain depressed and crushed for long days. But it wouldn't take him long to ask God's forgiveness, saying, "Praise be to God. No one is praised for an affliction except him." Meanwhile, Juri remained broken, feeling that she was responsible for giving birth to female children who quickly died.

The midwife slipped, and Mazloom was so absorbed by his memories that he would have fallen on top of her if he hadn't at the last minute grabbed onto a tree. Lami'a yelled at the same time as the thunder, insulting the devils who ambushed good people every time the sky grew dark. Mazloom thought she meant him, but he ignored her. He helped her get back on her feet and carried her bag for the rest of the way; her woolen wrap was soiled with mud.

When they entered the house, they heard Juri's screaming and choking. Lami'a said, "Heat me some water quickly," and by the light of the shaking lamp she started examining Juri and reassuring her.

"Don't be worried. Seek the help of al-Zahra, the mother of the Hassanayn.[5] Don't clench."

Although the room was cold, Juri was dripping with sweat.

"Push. Only a little while to go. Open your legs. Don't squeeze them together. Don't worry, the baby is coming at dawn, and dawn is soon, God willing. Come on, control yourself. Push. Keep going."

Just before five in the morning, a lump of blue flesh fell into Lami'a's palms, and after a moment the yelling increased. The two small legs were twisted together, so the midwife separated them to identify the baby's sex. Juri was still moaning and gnashing her teeth. The midwife wrapped the lump of flesh while Mazloom al-Sa'idi waited tight-lipped behind the door, his heart heavy with grief.

"Didn't I tell you it would be a daughter?"

Mazloom didn't answer; he was like someone who had fallen into a dark well. The midwife was about to hand him the little one when she heard the mother's voice. She returned to Juri and was surprised by the sight of another head. She guided it out. This one was smaller, and she didn't need to separate the baby's legs this time—they were open. She immediately called to Mazloom al-Sa'idi: "It is the son you were waiting for!"

---

5. Fatima al-Zahra: the daughter of the Prophet Mohammed and the mother of al-Hassan and al-Hussein.

He felt such strength that he almost fainted. The midwife cleaned the baby's body, and when she had finished, she wrapped him in a soft fabric and handed him to Mazloom al-Sa'idi. As soon as he held his son, he broke into tears. At that moment, Juri was quiet from exhaustion. Lami'a started cleaning her forehead and sprinkled her face with rose water, moaning verses from the Holy Qur'an. Juri slowly opened her eyes and looked at Mazloom, who was breathless as he hugged the child. Meanwhile, the other lump of flesh was quiet, as if she hadn't come to life or as if she already realized that from that moment on she was surplus.

Looking at the male child, Mazloom al-Sa'idi said, "His name is Nadir."

"What about the girl?" the midwife asked him, and, as if remembering a forgotten thing, he said, "The girl? I leave it to you. Choose the name you want."

Without hesitation, the midwife said, "Her name is Nadia. After my daughter."

When my father had been struggling in the mud holding the midwife's hand, he had thought that every female birth was equivalent to death. He was sure that if there had been a male baby among the four births, that son would have held on to life. But the days deceived my father, for he himself died a year after our birth. I survived, and a male in the family died.

WHAT COULD I DO with the lengthening hours? Time had slowed down. I had nothing to do. My days in Amman were quiet, like still water. But Nadia stirred it after her death, nailing me down in front of her memories. I wondered what came after this difficult birth.

My existence began there in that forgotten village of just a few hundred houses in Abu al-Khasib. From the first cry of my birth, my life was marked by neglect in favor of Nadir. Our house was small, with a courtyard separating its two rooms, and behind one of the rooms was a storage area. Our beds were made out of palm branches. In front of my mother's bed was a pile of blankets, pillows, and sheets. The floor was covered with woolen rugs on top of mats of palm leaves. The roofs were made of palm trunks and fronds covered with layers of dried mud; the walls were washed with gypsum. When we had just learned to walk, the government decided to build a grain-storage facility in the village. The compensation that my mother obtained allowed her to move to the center of the town. There I went to school and learned my first letters. Years later we heard that the storage facility was converted into a chemical factory, which would be destroyed in the Gulf War.

WHAT HAPPENED TO US? How did we cross those terrifying desert distances, fleeing to save our tortured souls? Why did Nadia have to die before she found a country that would shelter her? And why did the embassy refuse to repatriate her body to Iraq? Don't we have the right to be buried on the land of our ancestors? Does the president have the right to retain his grip even on the dead after having deprived them of joy during their lives? What can a powerless corpse do? It can't claim compensation for years burned out by the wars. Yet the president fears even corpses that are unable to object or resist. What about me? How am I going to end and in which land? I'm the one who dared to say "No." I then found myself adrift, leaving behind everything—my house, my memories, my grandmother, and Youssef, my childhood's dream. They planted him as a husband in my head, and I loved him. Or perhaps I only thought I loved him because there was no one else in my life. The last thing he said to me when he was handing me the passport was, "Don't waste time. Be ready at 8:00 p.m. Your permanent identity papers will reach you later on." He gave me a piece of paper. "Here is Hani's address. Do you remember him?" Yes, I remembered him. He was a Palestinian guy who had been in college with Youssef. I had met him a couple of times.

"Don't forget your new name, Samia Shahine Hassan. Remember your birth date—we had to make you forty-five years old to avoid the requirement for a male chaperone."

I took with me just a small clothing bag and another handbag with only a notebook, tissues, a pen, the passport, and a few aspirin. I wrapped my head in a black shawl and wore glasses so that I looked older. Youssef said good-bye to me quickly; he was still upset with me— or at least that was how it seemed to me.

On the wide desert road across thousands of miles, the car devoured the road and stole away my calm. I was in the backseat, sitting next to a woman with her child. Her husband was in the front, next to the driver. Some drivers were willing to report any suspicious behavior to the government, so I felt apprehensive about our driver. Drivers would first start by pulling a passenger into conversation about living conditions and the state of the country and then casually ask about the passenger's reasons for travel. I avoided taking part in the conversation.

I feigned sleep, but I couldn't spend twenty exhausting hours sleeping. After the driver had gossiped enough with the man and his wife and knew about their motives, he turned to me.

"I'm about to have surgery, and my father is waiting for me in Amman, where he has made arrangements for a hospital room," I told him. The woman wanted to know about my disease. I improvised the phrase "removing a growth near the liver," but I didn't take part in the follow-up comments about the diseases ravaging Iraqis, the scarcity of medication, and the high rates of cancer after the Gulf War. Every time we had to halt at checkpoints, my heart stopped, but I had to be patient and contain myself.

The wheels of the car were crushing my ribs, anxiety and fear overwhelming my dreams and expectations. Youssef's face was following me; he looked upset, insisting, "Remember the new name, Samia Shahine Hassan. I will join you after three or four months, as soon as I finish my training." (I knew military training never ended. It devoured the lives of youths, eating their dreams, until they suddenly found themselves in their forties.)

My grandmother's face took the place of Youssef's, insisting, "You are lying. You are not headed to Najaf." As I had held her hands, she had been certain that we would never meet again; if I hadn't been in such a hurry, she would have sewn me a talisman and hidden it in my breast. But there hadn't been that much time, so she had offered me a camel-bone necklace, placing it around my neck while saying, "It will bring you patience and luck."

In the car, I anxiously tried to be patient. Through the fogged glass, I saw a star sparkling in the dark night. A small window opened before me, and so I returned

again to my grandmother. I entered her distinctive room.
It was a special world. As soon as you crossed the threshold, you would notice the change in the atmosphere, a
mixture of scents—henna, incense, and mastic. Her mattress was on the floor, for she had refused to sleep on
the bed since the death of her husband. In the corner
across from her mattress was a thick woolen carpet that
she had made herself, placed on mats, and surrounded
by soft woolen pillows. On top of a small wooden table
near the bed was a copy of the Holy Qur'an. My grandmother was educated and literate, which was uncommon
because females of her generation and even the generation that came right after hers were usually illiterate. She
says that she completed the reading of the Qur'an when
she was nine. Her father was one of the students of the
Islamic learning center in Najaf, but he never finished
because he died from malaria. In her closet were a number of dresses, and in the lowest drawer she still kept
her wedding dress, a faded pistachio color embroidered
with white glittering beads. Next to it were a few objects
left by my grandfather: a rosary from al-Hussein, a silver cigarette box, and an oak cane with a serpent head.
Although my grandmother had not been preoccupied
with the past and wouldn't cry over it, she nevertheless
missed those days. She always used to repeat, "How is
it possible for life to go on without me? I lived it fully, a
simple, safe, and sweet life. Now wars have disfigured
life's beautiful face. The present doesn't mean much to
me; it just confuses me. Sometimes as an escape from it, I
think about the past, and that's enough."

I used to envy her. I envied the strength with which
she fought the hardships of life. The bright memories of

the past and her sense of humor never left her. She used to have difficulties with modern names, still calling the pillow *lulah*, the chair *sakmali*, and the medicine cabinet *sandagja*, and oftentimes she would finish her stories with the expression, "It was back then, in the days of plenty."

Someone was snoring in the car, and the image of my grandmother disappeared. I looked at the woman sitting next to me; she was deep in sleep. Fear of the unknown overwhelmed me. Time was slow; it weighed on my chest and suffocated me. My patience disintegrated even though the necklace my grandmother had given me encircled my neck. I swerved away to the furthest skies of the past, to where I had played in that wide street. I had snatched the sunflower seeds from al-Zayir Jabr's store, and then I had run away with the small black grains, holding them like a treasure. I had been flooded with pleasure when I succeeded in distracting al-Zayir Jabr and grabbed a handful. But the pleasure had disappeared when I realized that al-Zayir Jabr had turned a blind eye. I threw the small grains on the side of the street and hid under the blankets in my bed, ignoring my mother's calls to help her string beans. Hoping that she would stop calling, I feigned sleep, but she called me again and again. I suddenly felt her near my head. I refrained from moving or making noise to fool her, and the taste of the small stolen grains came back into my mouth. Then I needed to urinate but waited a little bit lest my mother called me again. Time pressured my bladder. I shriveled under the blankets and then did it in my bed.

The cold crept into my bones, and time was still slow. I plunged into distant memories to avoid my confused feelings. My mother's serene voice sprang up from the past, telling me on one of the afternoons during a forgotten year, "I threw your umbilical cord in the Tigris; you fell on the sand of its bank because I couldn't wait until I arrived back home." I had placed my chin between my palms while listening to her with clear eyes.

"I was with my neighbors washing clothes and dishes on the verge of the river. We had been laughing and joking when all of a sudden I cried out for help. My friends rushed to me, repeating prayers. They tried to take me back home, but you didn't wait, and you fell like a limp worm. Suddenly, the place turned into a festival of joyful cries. One of the women wrapped you in her woolen robe after she cut the umbilical cord and gave it to me. I threw it into the river. Then they took me home. This is how you came to life, easily and conveniently. I was hoping you would live with ease and comfort. But the river that witnessed your birth and preserved you from its treacherous currents took your father two months later. He was a skilled fisherman, and I just couldn't believe that he had drowned. They said that the strong current swept him away after his fishing boat capsized, but I still don't believe it. No one ever tried to find out the truth. The police were convinced by the witnesses, but the witnesses' motives were suspicious; they might have wanted to get rid of him because he was their only rival in the fish-marketing trade."

I knew my father only through photographs. Most of them were taken on the river among fishermen—he was usually holding a fish he had just caught, stretching the fishing net, standing on the shore. In some of the photos, he was with my mother. I wasn't nostalgic about him, for he was simply a picture in my imagination. But sweeping nostalgic emotions still drew me to my mother. I was still pressed by the desire to touch her fingers, to listen to her voice, to follow in her footsteps as I used to do in my childhood. She was a strong woman. She patiently faced the difficulties of raising me, and after my father's death, she refused to remarry, although she was still young. She lived under my uncle's protection for two years, and when he got married, she lived independently in a small house with my paternal grandmother, with whom I had been much closer. My mother was very busy securing our living, working until she died in a vegetable oil factory. When she died, I was in my second year of college in the Faculty of Arts.

My nostalgia was interrupted when the car stopped at a checkpoint. A soldier who couldn't have been more than twenty appeared at the window; he stared at our faces and looked at me. I forced a smile. He didn't search our belongings and didn't ask for anything. He gave his signal to the driver to move on. As the car crept forward, I shuddered. The checkpoint's lights retreated; once again we were plunged into the night's darkness. I stuck my face to the window glass. Nothing. The night was end-less, and the sky distant—no moon, not a single star. I felt as though we were in a dark tunnel with no end in sight. My soul flew ahead of me and over the border blockades, fleeing as though pursued by a hunter's bullet, going as high as it could in hopes that the bullet would miss the mark. Suddenly I was shaking, and my teeth were chat-tering. I pulled myself together, searching for strength. The checkpoints were endless: rapid questions and strange looks . . . cold . . . fear . . . heavy hours . . . until we reached Tribil, the last station.

When the driver asked me to get out of the car there, I was terrified, and my fear felt like sharp canine teeth. My throat dried up, and my lips hardened. I gripped the beads of the camel necklace, hoping that they would bring me good fortune. But my throbbing heart continued its agitated leaps, one after another. The most horrible moment was when I stood before the passport officer. He ordered me to wait after he took my passport. I looked around me; there was no place to sit. Passengers from other cars had taken all the chairs, and some remained standing. Exhausted, I leaned against the wall. I tried in vain to push away the black ideas devouring my spirit, sinking their talons deep into my heart. I could see the officers dragging me into a small room and taking turns interrogating me in the nastiest way. They would drive me back to the dark face of Baghdad. Then anonymous hands would grab me and drag me into a basement, where they would strip me of my clothes and fall upon me with whips and blows. Before I could scream from the horror of the anticipated pain, the passport officer yelled, "Samia Shahine Hassan!"

My heart stopped beating, and I couldn't make a sound. The call was repeated twice. My heart started beating again. I panicked as I ran to the window. The officer looked at me angrily. "Are you deaf?"

I couldn't believe it when he handed me the passport. I wasn't sure when or how I left that office. I was torn between joy and sorrow as the car continued on its way to the Jordanian border. I poked my face into the glass. Dawn had begun to steal in, and although I was out of danger, horrible thoughts still lay in wait for me. What if, as often happens, the security officers followed us and stopped the car out of suspicion? What if they found out about the false passport? Wouldn't it have been better to flee with a passport in my real name? Were things really as dangerous as Youssef thought when he had arranged for this passport? Perhaps. Anything was possible when our rights were lost and the state devoured our lives little by little.

The morning became brighter, but the beating of my heart and my breathing didn't return to normal until after the car finally crossed the al-Rouwaychid checkpoint. It was early morning, and a light rain drizzled on the window. I glanced at the black stone fields along the road and saw skeletons of old cars among the scattered vegetation. The land started waving up and down, and I recorded my first day in exile.

WHEN I SET FOOT IN AMMAN, I stretched to my full length and felt alive. Only a few hours earlier I'd been shrunken and scared, horrified, overcome by black thoughts. Getting out of the car was like a new birth, and I was taking my first steps. I took my bag to the nearest telephone booth and called Hani. His brother answered and said that Hani was in Naplouse, but that Youssef had called from Baghdad about me. After almost twenty minutes, a thin young man arrived, and I went to meet him.

"Are you looking for me?"

"Are you Huda?"

"Yes."

"I'm Hussam, Hani's brother."

We walked to his house. Umm Hani welcomed me with open arms as though she had always known me. She was a slightly plump woman in her fifties, elegant and with a silver tongue. She offered me a lemonade and then led me to another room. "You need to rest after the fatigue of the road."

I slept most of the day, but when I got up, my body was still exhausted; fear and the journey's length had sapped all of my strength. Over lunch, Hussam told me that he'd visited Baghdad twice, found it beautiful, and intended to study medicine there.

I stayed three days in Hani's home. With his mother's help, I then rented a small room above a carpentry workshop. I had to climb 120 steps to reach it, and it overlooked a street crowded with government offices and trade buildings.

On my first night there, I had insomnia. The landlady, Umm Ayman, had told me that before me, an Iraqi man and his wife had rented the place for more than a year. I tried in vain to forget the two bodies that had shared the same bed I was sleeping on now—this feeling was to become part of my exile. As soon as I pulled the blanket to my body, I would smell a strange odor, a mixture of old sweat and something like an old, rotten peach. Although Umm Ayman vowed that she'd washed and sterilized the blankets, I couldn't help thinking about the breath and odors of previous bodies. I had been accustomed to perfuming my bed with incense from Najaf every night before I went to sleep. It's a habit I had picked up from my grandmother; I would burn sticks of incense along with grains of clove. Holding the censer, I would walk around my bed so that I could sleep with a serene soul and body. Now, however, I needed time to get used to the new smells, the moist walls, the low ceiling, the small window overlooking the street. I came here with a ruined soul and broken hopes, so I had no choice but to adapt. From the first week of my arrival, I applied myself to exploring the city—its alleys and streets, its people and markets, its kiosks and bookstores. During the first three days, Hussam showed me the chief spots in Amman. Later I found the city's main library, where I would spend an hour or two reading. I had to resist the desire to buy books because I had to save what little money I had until Youssef's arrival in three months or four or five—I didn't know.

THE FIRST DIALOGUE I had with Youssef went as follows:

"This is Samia." (I gave the false passport name out of fear of intelligence agents.) "I hope I won't have to wait long until I see you."

"Don't worry. Just look after yourself."

"I miss you. I miss you all. How is Grandma?"

"She misses you a lot. She suggested renting your house in Baghdad; if this works out, I'll send you the rent money."

And the second conversation:

"You'll be getting your permanent identity papers soon."

"What about you?"

"Be patient a little bit more."

"Can I talk to my grandma?"

"She's not here. She went out with my mum to visit the Imam al-Kadhim. How can I reach you?"

"I don't know. I don't have a phone. I'm calling with a phone card."

"A card—what does that mean?" (Of course, no one in Iraq knew the phone card system.)

"It's a public phone where we use special cards; listen, I'm afraid it will cut off soon. I'll call later."

The third time was different:

"Did you receive your permanent ID?"

"Yes, the papers arrived along with the money."

"Samia, what's the matter with your voice?"

"I just have a cold."

"No, your voice is very sad."

"Do you remember my friend Nadia?"

"Nadia? Yes, I remember her."

"She was killed."

I pulled out the phone card right before I broke into tears.

NADIA AND I had to go our separate ways at the end of 1993. Her family had to leave Baghdad during the evacuation of those originally from the South who had fled their homes because of Desert Storm. Of all the cities in Iraq, Basra had suffered the greatest destruction because it was the only city along the route for both the lines of invasion into Kuwait and the lines of defeat coming back from there. After the death of thousands on the battlefields and along this "trail of death," the defeated troops who remained alive had returned from Kuwait. In Basra houses had been destroyed with their inhabitants inside; those who were able to had fled to Baghdad, Karbala, and Najaf, thinking that the capital and the holy places would be safer.

On her second visit to my home on Mount al-Hussein, Nadia had told me that when her family had returned to Basra, they couldn't find their house or even their old neighborhood. Both had been completely destroyed and become a dumping ground for garbage and waste. One of their acquaintances suggested that Nadia's family register their names on the list of those who had suffered damages from the war. But other people warned them that doing so was useless because no Iraqi ever received compensation. The people of Basra were particularly stigmatized for their hostility to the regime because the 1991 uprising had originated there. This meant that in response to any request for compensation, the intelligence services would unearth files, sources, origins, and relatives—not to offer compensation, but to find out whether the requester had any connection with the uprising. Nadia's uncle had been killed in the first days of the rebellion in front of Nadia's house while he was trying to remove a corpse from their threshold. For this act, he was considered against the regime, and the family had to take refuge with one of their relatives. Then Nadir was hired as a driver by Hamid Kalla.

AT THE REFUGEE OFFICE, the waiting line only grew longer and longer. It would organize and dissolve, then gather and dissolve again. After almost an hour, an officer appeared and from the bars of the closed door called some names. He handed people notices that their appointments were postponed. Some grumbled and walked away, but a fifty-year-old man standing next to a woman holding a child said, "Please, I have been on the waiting list for six months. This is the fourth time I've been postponed."

The officer continued distributing notices of new appointments as though he hadn't heard anything. The man asked again, "Is there anyone I can talk to?"

His question was lost amid the child's crying, and the officer disappeared into the building without answering. He also didn't hear my voice when I called him, or perhaps he heard but ignored me. Some women were sitting on the ground and on the sidewalk. Every one of them was pondering her suffering. My back hurt, so I sat down next to a woman with a pale face. She looked at me and asked for some water from the bottle I was holding.

Any occasion is an opportunity for us to confess to a stranger; we Iraqis do not need reasons or introductions when our hearts can no longer bear the weight of our tragedy. Thus, as soon as the woman returned the bottle, she started to tell her story. "I have been coming to the Refugee Office for five months now. My daughter is a medical doctor; she left Iraq before I did, and I have followed her. She left through the services of clandestine immigration to shorten the time and the troubles of waiting here. She should have arrived four months ago in Germany, where her father is waiting for her. He has been a refugee there for two years. But she didn't wait for him to send her official papers. She paid a lot of money, but since then I haven't heard anything from her. She hasn't arrived in Germany, and she hasn't been in touch with me."

I asked, "What have they done for you here at the Refugee Office?"

She bowed her head silently. I looked at her emaciated face and her dry lips as I listened to her response. "How should I know? I don't even know the office my daughter dealt with. I arrived in Amman three days before she left, and she assured me then that she would arrive safely in

Germany. Here I am, waiting. I have lost it all: daughter, husband, and homeland."

We were eventually admitted to the office. The corridor leading to the waiting room was three feet wide and paved with dark tiles. The last step up to the main door to the waiting area looked tortuous, as though to remind us that the road we were about to take would be endlessly long and twisted. The only waiting area was too small for the number of applicants. The children were shouting and fighting over three plastic toys: who would get to ride the horse first, who would get to crawl inside the belly of the goose, who would get to play with the blocks. One of the children snatched some blocks from another, and a lopsided fight started between a fat little bully and a skinny, scared child.

A few men leaned against the wall, and some women sat on large stones scattered randomly throughout the room. Others would walk in and out as though looking for something they had lost. There was only one story circulating among the people, though with different details—the flight from hell and the lack of work opportunities in Amman. As soon as I sat next to someone, I would find myself listening to that person's story, which was also my own. From time to time, the officer Abou al-Abd emerged to call out a few file numbers or to read aloud some instructions. All eyes would be on him before he even said anything. The hours lengthened, the children shouted endlessly, and the stories circulated.

"My son emigrated two years ago. He got in touch with me only once when I was in Baghdad. I've been waiting nine months. All I know about him is that he is in Michigan, and his phone is out of service." The woman wrapped in her black woolen cloak continued, "Could the phone possibly be out of service this whole time?" Her tears were visible.

The young woman sitting next to her asked, "What did they tell you here?"

With her fingers intertwined, the first woman said, "I met with them a month ago, and they gave me an appointment today. What do you think? Will they be able to find him?"

Abou al-Abd came out from his small office. He read aloud the file numbers. A few men and women moved off, their children following them; among them was the woman who hadn't had any news from her son. The rest continued to ruminate over their stories.

"Would you believe it? I'm a professor," said a slightly frail man wearing medical glasses. "I spent twenty years teaching and researching—imagine, a professor, and my salary can't meet my family's needs."

"But how did you manage to leave Iraq? Persons with your scientific rank are not allowed to travel. Did you flee?"

The professor smiled and adjusted his glasses. "No, I bribed a doctor to make a report saying that I have been diagnosed with heart disease. I left on a medical pretext; then my family joined me. It's all about bribery."

"I sold everything," another man said, "the house, the car, the furniture. Life had become unbearable; no other hope was left for us except to look for a decent life away from the humiliation and disease. But, believe me, the most beautiful country will not be able to replace Iraq, despite all its destruction."

"My story is worse," said a third person. "I have been condemned to death in absentia. I lost my self-control and spat on one of the party members in my neighborhood, and, worse, I insulted the president as well."

"And they didn't cut out your tongue?"

"After I calmed down, I realized what was going to happen to me and fled just before they caught me. But I was right."

Before the man could finish his story, Abou al-Abd showed up again to read new numbers and to say that the rest were to be postponed. He smiled, saying, "Sorry, but we need to check some intelligence information about some of you. You can come back next Sunday."

This was the third time my appointment had been postponed since I had filed an application consisting of twenty-six questions. The application required a strong memory and details about family members, relatives, and their addresses, school years, and years of graduation. My permanent identity papers had been sent to me at Hani's address via one of the drivers working on the route line between Baghdad and Amman.

I returned to my room feeling ambivalent. It was one thirty. I took out leftovers and warmed them up. No one was around to talk to. I threw my body on the bed, not caring about the smells. I sank into a terrible void, and I found myself wandering the streets of Kadhimiya, strolling through narrow, twisted alleys.

I could see women on their doorsteps staring at me and whispering. I passed them on my way to the herb shops: the scents of incense, spices, cardamom, and nuts tickled my nose. I bought some incense and entered the shrine of Moosa al-Kadhim. I held onto the window's silver grate, breathing in the shrine's spiritual perfume. The visitors' prayers and exaltations rose and fell, purifying me and giving me peace. Women showered their offerings over the crowd's heads; cries of joy rang out. I was struck by the weeping women who were holding on to the illusion of fulfilled prayers. Their grieving hearts were aching for missing children and missed husbands, including those without graves. I could see emaciated men with vacant glances standing in the corners. Young girls were reciting silent prayers, hoping the saint would heal their troubles and fill their hearts with faith and hope. I could see children dedicated to the saint, wretched beggars, women with shriveled bellies, sheikhs who had lost their children and years of their lives, fingers clinging to the grates, shivering and seeking refuge. I could hear wailing, smothered sighs, prayers for protection, crying.

One of the custodians, who was wearing the green-tissue strips of hope on his wrist, called hoarsely, "May the saint Abu al-Jawadayn protect you from all evil." Another one asked, "Any vows?" A third one wrapped a child in cotton cloth in his father's arms and read the sura of the dawn.

Bodies were pressed against bodies, and everyone was calling, praying, and seeking help and protection. Among the exalted voices and the weeping eyes, I could see Youssef's face, but in a flash it was wrenched away. I slipped among the crowd to try to hold on to him, calling, "Youssef, Youssef!" I woke up, not knowing if what I had seen was a night vision or a daydream.

I carried myself to the phone booth and dialed. No one answered. Perhaps they were out visiting or shopping. I tried again in the afternoon and an hour later. I called again and again at different times for a week. What had happened to Youssef? Where was my aunt? Why was no one responding? I reassured myself by thinking up many excuses—service interruptions, for instance, because telephone service was often interrupted in Iraq. Since the war, the central telephone lines had been only half functional because the embargo still continued on some merchandise and equipment. It was foolish to think that the government wanted to lift the embargo; it wanted to maintain the suffering of those who had resisted the regime after the liberation of Kuwait. The uprising then had been the largest and most widespread the country had ever witnessed. That is why people in the southern districts were still drinking polluted water. It was a collective punishment. The internal blockade surpassed the blockade imposed by the superpowers.

On the eighth day, I got up early. I had a glass of milk and left for the Refugee Office. The sky was covered with white and dark clouds, but the fresh air was filled with the smell of flowers. As usual, we stood waiting until the doors would be opened. The woman I had previously sat next to was sitting in the same place near the sidewalk. I sought a remote corner in order to avoid asking her what had happened to her daughter. After almost a half hour, an officer appeared. He began asking and answering questions; then he let in a large number of people. We spread out inside the room and in the narrow yard. Time stretched from hour to hour, and we filled it with the stories that had become familiar and boring. The doctor's mother was among the next group that entered. As soon as she saw me, she walked toward me as though we were old friends. Then, without my asking, she told me that her daughter had called her from Malaysia and said that she had been arrested along with others who had entered the country illegally. Her eyes glistened with tears as she told me about her daughter. "Life is very tough, and the treatment is bad; they treat them as though they were robbers, making them sleep on the floor with just a blanket under their bodies and another one as a cover. Their problem now depends on meeting with the United Nations delegate."

"Huda Abdel Baqi."

I jumped from my seat without excusing myself to the woman. I walked behind Abou al-Abd through a narrow corridor. He asked me to enter the room and returned to his business. I sat before a young woman whose face was without makeup or expression. There was a computer in front of her. She began asking me questions as she typed my answers. I admitted to her that my passport was false and that my name was Huda Abdel Baqi, as it showed on my papers and citizenship certificate. I gave her a precise narrative of facts and events and answered all the questions concerning studies, home, number of living and dead relatives, dates long past, and how and where I lived here. She asked me to draw a map of my home and a few other things that in my opinion were not important. She ended our meeting by stressing that asylum was not my right, but only a temporary solution; everyone who came here should know that. After that meeting, I bore the number 2426. When I left the Refugee Office, the atmosphere was colder, and dark clouds were thickening. I halted at a phone booth. I dialed, every part of my body hanging onto this silent machine, waiting for a voice. Just as before, no one picked up, although I let it ring a long time, holding on as though entangled in its wires. I tried again; perhaps Baghdad would awake from its silence. No one replied; no one came. I couldn't travel there.

THE HANDS OF MY BEDROOM CLOCK had stopped. I checked its battery to see if it had shifted out of place. I hung it back on the wall, but it was still the same. I thought of buying a new battery and went to bed without eating anything. I seemed to be diving into a void. Many questions started clamoring in my head. Why wasn't anyone answering? What had happened to Youssef? He should have finished his additional military service a month ago. Was he still trying to pay the heavy taxes required to travel?[6] My aunt had been trying to keep him away from the wars and their calamities. Youssef had been tired of war, and I knew that desperation had been eating his heart. He had often told me that he couldn't live in a country where war would only hatch out more wars and where he had to guard his life lest he be killed or driven to suicide. We'd discussed his leaving Iraq for a long time before he was convinced; he was very opposed to the idea of Iraqi migration. What was delaying him, then? My thoughts went in vicious circles, asking the same questions, setting up excuses, creating illusions that I believed, until I felt dizzy. I stood up and washed my face, but my body was still tense. Nadia's notebook caught my attention. I grabbed it and started reading.

6. During the 1990s, the Iraqi government made it very difficult for Iraqis to travel abroad. They had to pay heavy taxes, around four hundred thousand Iraqi dinars (anywhere from three to four hundred US dollars), to be able to travel.

On that unfortunate cold morning, the atmosphere was dense with the smell of death. A few cars were parked in front of the big prison gates in Basra, where guards with jackal eyes patrolled and kept surveillance from the observation towers. People's faces were pale and their eyes expectant, their lips locked and filled with anger. Distressed and defeated women wore black woolen cloaks that blew open in the wind, revealing their humble clothing and wasted bodies. Men with heads swathed in *koufiya* smoked compulsively, their eyes red and blank. All eyes looked toward the iron gate. No one dared to ask questions. The guards were fully armed, ready to attack. They looked at us with disdain, although it was they who were despicable.

My uncle and I had sought refuge near the car that would transport Nadir's body. To keep myself from surrendering to tears and stop my spirit from shattering, I bit my parched lips fiercely till they almost bled. I pressed on my throat to suppress my cries. Memories transfixed me with quick images and flashes, deluding me, bringing closer a childhood that had flown away from me. Deceptive images danced in my head: me playing with a cotton doll that Nadir might come and snatch away in a moment. I would follow him with insults; then he would turn and hit me. I would cry, so he would suggest that we go to the garden to collect mulberry and pomegranate flowers. This image disappeared and gave way to another. Here was Nadir plagued by puberty, sticking actresses' photos on the walls and collecting tapes of modern music. Under his pillow he would hide papers. I suspected they were love letters or love poems for a woman he hadn't met yet.

Cold wind slapped our tired faces, carrying with it the fates of the murdered. An officer came out. Shaking steps hastened, and tears petrified. He read aloud the names of our dead, every name preceded by the word *traitor*. He requested that only one person from each family enter to sign the acknowledgment of the body's receipt. I was frozen in place, my teeth chattering. My uncle entered with some of the men. They all disappeared behind the gate, leaving the rest of us to our sadness. No one wept. No one cried out. Everything was forbidden, and the silence whipped our dismayed souls. After a little while, the coffins came out, one after the other. They were put on top of the cars and went their separate ways.

My uncle sat next to the driver, and I sat next to my mother in the backseat. The way to holy Najaf was long and hard. I felt as though I were swallowing fire; it ran down my throat and burned my intestines. I didn't dare look at my mother after we picked her up. I feared that if I looked at her, I would hurt her even more deeply.

My uncle, the driver, and I had carried the coffin and gone home to pick her up. I waited in the car while my uncle walked into the house. The neighbors stood on their thresholds or stared from their windows; no one dared to share our grief openly because everything could be observed; every place was filled with furtive eyes and dirty hands formulating secret reports.

My mother walked out with bowed head, holding my uncle's hand for fear of falling. She didn't look at the car's roof; perhaps she wanted to delay her cries so that she wouldn't break down in front of everybody. I was surprised that she didn't cry out and didn't say anything till we left Basra. Then she unleashed all the cries that had been pent up inside her; she slapped her cheeks and ripped the pocket of her tunic. I tried to hold her, but her deep sadness had exploded like a volcano and gave her incredible strength.

The driver stopped and turned to her: "Say nothing will happen to us except what Allah has decreed for us."[7] Still she continued weeping and crying throughout the long journey. I began sobbing along with her; then I calmed myself and looked out the window, hoping to find a way to save my exhausted soul. Alongside vast deserted areas stretched the marshes, their banks dotted with black-and-white birds; the small birds were the size of starlings, and the big ones the size of crows or storks.

My mother's cries became increasingly sharp and high. She began hitting the door of the car unconsciously when suddenly a strangely shaped bird crashed into the windshield. The driver, who had been imploring my mother to stop crying, jumped back startled, and the car swerved. He stopped the car and yelled angrily, "You see, we could have died, all of us, in the blink of an eye. Thank God the road is empty at this time; otherwise, it could have been a disaster."

My uncle leaned over the seat and put his palm on my mother's head, saying, "Weeping will not bring the dead back. Please, the car was about to roll over."

7. Qur'an IX, 51.

My mother stopped crying—not because of what my uncle had said, but because she didn't want Nadir to die twice.

The car devoured the road at a tremendous speed, as though consuming the earth. None of us objected to the driver's crazy speed. From time to time, I heard my mother's sighs and her silent, burning weeping; then I would look out the window again. The road stretched out with distant trees, scattered spikes, mineral ponds, enclosed fields, and herds of cows and sheep. From afar there loomed buildings sunk in fog, and I could see men walking with knee-high boots along little streams and freshly plowed land. A car carrying a bier occasionally sped past.

When we arrived at Khan al-Nass, two other cars were already there, each with a coffin on its roof. We recognized some of the faces that had been with us at the big prison gate. A few men got out. They had tea and smoked, and the women washed the dust of tragedy from their faces. Then we continued the journey.

In vain, I tried to escape Nadir's face, to rein in memory's willfulness and conceal my pain, hoping that doing so would lighten my sadness. I withdrew into a painful shell. Memory's knives cut into my head, though, taking me to my childhood, and I could see myself running behind Nadir.

Okra branches stung us, so we ran into the grapevine trellis; then we walked among the sesban trees, stripping their tender leaves. Butterflies hovered around the flowers. Nadir caught one of them; he held it between his thumb and his index finger. When he released it, nothing remained on his fingers except a light ash. We advanced farther and farther into the garden, fearing the guard would catch us trespassing. I found a bird with yellow fluff still on its tender flesh. Nadir grabbed it from my hands and looked at the highest point of the peach tree from which it had just fallen. He suggested climbing the tree, then put the bird in his pocket and climbed. He placed the bird inside the nest while the mother hovered around angrily. Before he came down, he picked a few peaches and threw them to me. As soon as he set his feet on the ground, the guard whistled. We ran away, terrified that he would whip us. When we were out of the garden, we threw ourselves on the ground, breathless, convulsing with loud laughter. Suddenly we were surprised by the guard's steps. We cried from fright, but he didn't hit us as we'd feared. He even let us take the peaches but warned us to keep away from his master's garden and insulted our fathers and grandfathers. We ran away crying.

My mother was crying out at the top of her hoarse voice when the dome of Imam Ali loomed nearer.

"I came to you, my imam, O father of the Hassanayn. This is your grandson. They killed him."

She was crying painfully, and the driver didn't interfere this time. My mother beat her face, which was covered in burning tears, but I had to search for my tears and found that I had none. Perhaps they had turned to stone inside me, or perhaps fate had hidden them somewhere to save them for dark days to come.

The car was moving slowly. Burial processions were leaving the place of the imam, and other people were getting through Bab al-Taous, spreading out toward the vast cemetery, accompanied by the sounds of continuous lamentation.[8] There were two funeral processions ahead of us, and many behind. We entered the cemetery through the gate leading to the burial offices. My uncle got out of the car and went into the offices; after a few minutes, he came out with the grave digger. My mother continued her painful sobbing; her heart seemed to be breaking with every cry. I wished I could cry like her to empty my soul of its pain at the loss of my twin. I begged for tears from my eyes and cries from my throat, but in vain.

We drove through narrow streets amid tombs and headed toward the family cemetery. After three hundred yards, we stopped, stupefied. Before me stretched an infinite number of tombs, tombs as far as the eye could see. When had the cemetery's womb grown so enormous? How did all these people die? Who had driven them to a fate that could have been delayed? It was amazing how death's machinery could work with such incredible speed. Tall tombs, layers on top of layers . . . marble tombs, low tombs, stone tombs, tombs made of baked bricks and of sandstone . . . tombs in the form of houses that the poor could not afford. Those with money had fancy tombs with pictures of their owners on the decorated doors. Martyrs occupied a large area in the cemetery. In pictures of them, their eyes uttered the burning question: "Why?" No one could answer that question. Some tombs were obliterated, forgotten by their people. Others were

8. Bab al-Taous: one of the gates of the holy city of Najaf.

new, and yet others were still being carved. No peace in Najaf's cemetery. The grave diggers' hands were always busy, and their livelihood would prosper as long as the wars had no end.

Some funeral processions halted next to us. The lamentations had never stopped: some women were crying and beating their chests, others were beating their heads and rending their cheeks—their tired faces sharing the same misfortunes and looking equally sad and devastated. The grave diggers were digging up the soil and carrying the corpses they would cover with sand, while the beggars hovered near.

We remember Death only when we enter cemeteries or when he approaches. Then we remove our masks and shrink away. We beg him to forgive us, to give us a respite just to settle past accounts, but Death doesn't pay attention. Undaunted by our supplications, he continues on. Everyone has his hour except the betrayed ones—war victims and the innocents.

My mother insisted on opening the coffin to take a last look at the boy who had delighted his father when he had come into the world. Where are you, Father? Do you remember that rainy night and the bitter cold? You were very sad and upset when the midwife told you of my birth, but as soon as Nadir came a few minutes after me, you felt your good fortune. You didn't get to enjoy it, though. Nadir and I used to crawl together toward you to get close to your warm lap. You would take him into your arms and give him so many cuddles and kisses, but ignore my fingers playing with your toes. I didn't cry despite my disappointment. Perhaps I hid my tears for some other time. And you left

us, despite the joy you felt before
to speak. Here you sleep in this cem
grave is being dug next to yours.

The grave digger's voice rose as I
keep things discreet. Don't you see ho
him in?"

How did my mother's fingers get the
lift the coffin's tightly closed cover? (Such a precaution
was amazing: did they fear their victims so much?)

The grave digger had come out of the hole and
was trying to grab my mother. My uncle tried to calm
her down, but her fingers were ferocious. I suddenly
found myself helping her to lift the cover, but as soon
as we removed it, we were consumed and paralyzed
by surprise. The corpse was not my brother, Nadir!

The last sentence was written at the top of an empty
page, as though Nadia wanted to catch her breath or
wanted to start a new chapter after remembering every
terrifying detail. I was turning the page when Umm
Ayman knocked on my door.

Nadia's notebook was still in my hands when I
opened the door. Umm Ayman sat down on the room's
only chair, looking into corners as if she had never seen
them before. I let her scan the walls; her eyes fell on a pile
of books on the small table; then she looked at the notebook and asked, "What are you reading?"

Although I knew she didn't care about reading and
had come to collect the rent, I answered, "I'm reading a
diary."

She opened her mouth in surprise, showing a gap in
her teeth. "Do you keep a diary?"

said casually, "No, it's the diary of my friend who passed away a few days ago."

She replied, patting her thigh, "May God have mercy upon her and all of us; we all share the same worries."

All of a sudden she asked me an unrelated question. "Have you found a job?"

I had bargained with her about the rent and had promised her that I would give her an increase as soon as I found a job. But days had passed, and I didn't have any energy for work.

"No, I haven't found one." I pulled the rent from under my pillow. "I knocked twice at your door, but no one was there; please take this."

Her features smoothed into a mask of kindness. "I came to inquire about you, not to ask for the rent." But as soon as I passed her the money, she grabbed it and slipped it in her pocket.

When she walked out, I sank into a deep depression, wondering, "How am I going to survive with only the little I have left?" But I didn't think deeply about the answer; I returned to Nadia's notebook to find out what had happened after they discovered the strange body.

After the initial shock, we carefully examined the corpse. Although the face had lost all of its features because of the torture—burns, gouged-out eyes, and mutilated lips—the white hair confirmed that a mistake had been made. My mother stood up, terrified. She looked around and cried commandingly, "Look for the owners of the cars that came with us."

My uncle hurried to the north side, and I ran behind my mother toward the west side, where groups were piling up sand on their dead. Our feet sank into the smooth, shifting sand and stones between the ruined tombstones, while the grave digger guarded the corpse.

"Stop!" my mother yelled in a breaking voice. Heads turned toward her. She looked miserable. Perhaps they thought she was deranged; they continued pouring the sand as though they hadn't heard anything. She yelled again and again, walking toward the grave that was still open.

"Listen to me carefully. The body I found in the coffin is not that of my son. Perhaps there is a mistake."

My uncle joined us and continued, "Didn't you come with us from that big prison?"

They immediately stopped pouring the sand and started digging up the grave. A woman in the crowd said, "Didn't I ask you to check it?"

No one answered. The grave digger objected, warning about the authorities, but no one listened to him amid the chaotic wailing and general cacophony. I sought refuge behind my mother, drawn by the smells of death and the sounds of lamentation emerging from the depths of the cemetery. My mother started running in different directions, looking for coffins and corpses. The others had identified their body just by looking at its face.

A voice came from another corner, "We have three legs here."

My mother ran with wild eyes and stricken heart. My uncle and I followed her. We made our way through the crowd surrounding the coffin, which revealed a dismembered man with a third leg packed among his limbs. At this point, the grave digger came and grabbed my uncle's shoulder, "What should I do? You are disrupting my work!"

My uncle said, "Go ahead and bury the body, and you will get your pay."

My mother collapsed near the open tomb while the grave digger covered the wrong corpse quickly, ignoring the funeral rituals because we knew the body wasn't ours. We spent that night in the shrine, and at dawn we returned to Basra. During the journey, my mother was silent except to answer questions or comments from others. Sometimes she muttered, seeking answers to the question running through all our minds: Where was Nadir's body?

I was also torn by other questions, thinking of my twin soul.

No doubt they tortured you. Perhaps they gouged out your beautiful eyes? Did you weaken at the last moment? Did you scream, asking for mercy from those whose hearts would never know mercy? Or did your strong body finally become numb to the pain? Did they blindfold your eyes? Or did they make you see yourself get shot and enjoy the look of fear on your face? How did your soul depart, my twin? How many moments did your last breath linger? What was the last image you saw? Was it my mother? Was it me? Or was it the executioner? I'm afraid they dismembered your body while you were still alive. What a beautiful body you had!

Between one question and another, my soul was screaming: "Where is Nadir's body?"

I HAD PLENTY OF TIME, but I wasn't doing anything. My days moved like a tortoise with flabby legs. I spent that time doing nothing, either in my room or the Refugee

Office or wandering around town, talking to myself because I had no one else to talk to. After plunging into Nadia's diary, I stopped going to Amman's library. I was feeling burdened and confused. A longing-for Baghdad dug deeply into my heart. Time was slow. I spent long hours looking at the corners and ceiling of my room, although I knew nothing was there. My head was stuffed with memories. Youssef's face and my grandmother's alternated in my head, consuming me. The alleys I had walked in Baghdad shone in my memory. I was drawn to the ebb and flow of the Tigris, on whose banks I had been born. Large banks, sweet clover, Indian fig and spinach, polished rocks, myrtle trees flanking the fences of the houses—all exhaled their fragrance in the corners of my memory and colored it with the henna of love. My memory would make its way to the Shourja Market crowded with customers on feast and holy days. The scents of herbs and spices would spread out from the market and tickle noses: pepper, essence of rose, aniseed, nutmeg, henna, rose water, pomegranate shell, and kohl of Mecca. I wouldn't know which of us was enticing the other, the memory or me. What a crowded memory, moving in a flash from one place to another. At one moment I would again be in Kadhimiya, wandering its streets, walking through its markets. Then I would enter Imam Moosa al-Kadhim's shrine through the al-Murad Gate. Women would be buying a miracle product for their problems: a mixture made out of dried grapes, chickpeas, and sweet citrus. I would wander about with the people, filling myself with the good smells, passing my hand along the fence. Different-colored tissues and strings would be knotted around the window in the hope that the imam would untie the knots and remove the sorrow. Hands would be lifted in supplication; wishes and tears would be pouring out as people wept. The gate-keeper would distribute pieces of green tissue that a visitor could wrap around his wrist to seek blessings and mercy. After a quick glance, I would swerve from the tumultuous crowd and walk through the north gate toward Sarbadi Market, where the shops were filled with merchandise: rosaries, woolen wraps, and *koufiya*, prayer rugs and handmade quilts, coffee sold in small cups. Bracelets and earrings, necklaces and silvery rings, rubies, wedding clothes decorated with ribbon, large candles hanging in front of the shops like chandeliers. I lit those candles in my memory so that the alleys would shine from their glow. They led me to the Café of the Captain on the other side of the Tigris, where I would meet Youssef. Today, though, in exile, I had no captain, and I could not steer my boat as I wished. My days were made of grief and vigils on plat-forms unattended by lovers. I was swept away by the vio-lent longing for memories of fleeting rendezvous, stolen kisses, and the fever of entangled fingers. The first meet-ing I had with Youssef was outside the family house, and our first date had been at the Café of the Captain. I had worn a short-sleeved blue dress and styled my hair loose along my shoulders, strutting in high heels like a princess, giving myself royal airs. My grandmother had given us her blessing while busy with her rosary: "Tonight is Saint Zakariyya's, when prayers are answered; visit the shrine of the prophet Elias before you go anywhere else."[9]

9. The shrine of the prophet Elias is said to be on the Tigris River in Baghdad.

There on the bank women had carried votive offerings, their wishes wandering on their lips and their hearts full of faith. The shrine of Elias had been full of visitors and guests carrying platters filled with gifts. Boats loaded with women and children had glided along the river. The bank had swarmed with fishermen, salesmen, and visitors. Lighted candles attached to palm-tree trunks had been floating in the Tigris.

I had said to Youssef, "Let's ask the saint for what we want; the doors of the sky are open today."

With difficulty we had walked down to the carnival. We had grabbed a myrtle branch and a candle and made our way through the crowd, walking hand in hand until we arrived at the Café of the Captain, looking for peace and exhorting our hearts to joy. Youssef had looked at me and asked about the wish buried in my heart, although we both knew one another's wish. It was a wish that we renewed each year, but that would not come true, for the war would suck the sap of love from Youssef's heart, stealing many years of his life. Sometimes I would hardly recognize him when he became violent for little, if any, reason. His mother would remain silent until he had returned to his peaceful nature and asked her pardon.

"It is the war, Mother. I'm not the same man."

"My son, why don't you get married? You and Huda love each other."

He had raised his hand toward her. "Do you want me to beget fodder for the next wars?"

He often said that he didn't know how he had carried a gun or pressed the trigger, and he sometimes fell into a depression merely thinking of the soldiers he might have killed. Once, while watching a program about the war, I had tried to pull him out of the abyss into which he had fallen upon seeing the constantly broadcast scenes. He had yelled at me: "You didn't experience what the soldiers did! How difficult it is to see a human laughing, singing, sobbing, remembering, complaining, and dreaming and then suddenly scattered into burned pieces! The head is no longer a head, and the heart is no longer a heart—just spattered blood or a charred body or severed limbs that we cannot gather. Unfortunate is the one who does not die instantly!"

His appearance had changed when he was talking about the war, and his eyes had flared red. I had said to him, "Let us not repeat these stories that have become a mere memory, a thing from the past," but he had continued, his voice dripping with pain.

"Life's sweetest years are lost in wars. We fought with fear, but with courage too. We were afraid during the fierce battles, but we were also filled with courage because we had to be. But it was a courage devoid of will. To kill a man—a man like you, directing his weapon to preserve his own life, just as you do—means that you are reducing your own humanity. When the two of you are good at shooting, you are just prolonging the regimes that drive the nation's children to the fires."

While he was talking, I remained silent and sad. But his violent moments quickly disappeared. Youssef had excused himself and returned to normal. He had looked at me and said, "What did you do to your hair? I like it as it is, untidy, not styled."

I said, "When I don't do my hair, I look like an idiot, and this pleases you?"

He had laughed and replied with a loving malice, "Who said you are not?"

I'd pretended to be upset, so he'd made peace with me, caressing my hand and fondling my fingers. I'd felt at that moment a strange feeling of joy. Then he'd added, "In this world, madness is the only way to freedom."

I hadn't wanted to argue with him because he was visibly sad, which I attributed to what he was suffering, given what was happening in the country—the psychological pressure and the difficulty of living a dignified life. We were talking about things we didn't fully understand and were unable to express as we wished. He had pressed my fingers again and said, "I know what you're thinking in your little head, and I realize how patient you've been. I love you, and nothing will ever shake that love, but love is not enough these days. It is important to preserve this love; as for the rest, let's leave it to the future."

And here were those days, my beloved. They came and went, stripping everything and crushing hope, pulling it by the roots from the land and casting it out of the garden of love.

> I wished for an age when I could love you
> And how many times the heart was tempted by the
>   love of the seas
> But your love is a long journey
> And the days of my life are short nights
> If I became the ruins of a star on the horizon,
> It would be enough that you are the orbit.

With these verses by the poet Farouk Jouweida, Nadia started a different chapter in which she talked about the impossible love affair that we had never discussed in Baghdad and that I hadn't wanted to press her about. Our most important concern then had been the loss of our lives under the pressure of the siege, and, later, exile exhausted what was left of our dreams. She had told me once, "I'm looking for my 'Emir,' for a speck in a stormy sea. It is my heart's wound. You will find out about it one day. Then your curiosity will be satisfied, but now let us think about a way out of suffering." At the time, we were sitting in Amman's Hashemite Square, a few days after we had met in Abdali. She was still as secretive as before. Neither of us knew that her heart's confessions would come after her sudden tragic death. I plunged with her into the furious sea of her confessions.

> My prince, my Emir, I write to you from my second month in exile. I know that my letters haven't reached you yet, but I write hoping they will find their way to you one day. My heart tells me that you are still alive and that you are somewhere in the world. I don't blame you for your absence—perhaps you are in a pit where angels have no access, facing a torture more than humans can bear, or perhaps you are hiding in a country where no one will recognize you. I can believe anything except that you are among the dead. Do you know, since you disappeared, I have been lost in thought, a prey to distraction? Some people even think that I have gone mad. That's all right—I'm crazy about you. I feel we connected and that we'll meet again one day. Where? I don't know; perhaps on a boat smuggling immigrants or on an expected road. When? I don't know; it might take some time. And perhaps we'll forget, or we'll pretend to forget after we get older, or

perhaps each of us will have chosen a companion and been faithful to him or her; then our meeting will be pale and cold. No, no, I'm just rambling . . . Forgive me. You are my lover and my compass if I get lost. I will definitely meet you and finish the journey with you. Wait for me, Prince! I will find you, or our paths will cross, even if it happens after our bodies are gone.

This letter had no date, and neither did the others. I read the second letter.

I wonder, my prince, when did my hand slip away from yours? I don't know the answer. Memory alone leads me to you. I remember there was a big crowd, and the world around was filled with noise. We were sitting in one of the garden corners on Sindibad Island, drinking cocoa and planning our life far from the destruction befalling the people. Perhaps a thousand times we built the castles of our love while crowds of children jumped, radiant in their feast clothes. I told you, "Look at them; they are reenacting our childhood," and I told you about my childhood and how on the feast's eve I used to sleep with my palms covered with henna and wrapped in tissue till the morning. Then I would get up and wash my hands and get dressed before anyone got up. I would walk to Nadir's bed and wake him so that we could get our feast-day presents and hurry to the carnival rides. We didn't plan for difficult days because life hadn't yet disclosed its ugly face. We were propelled by our feelings. And when a cloud appeared, our hands intertwined till it passed peacefully. No peace after today, though, my prince.

Memories of our childhood have faded away, and our souls are wandering aimlessly, lost, chased by the fear of the unknown and the search for security. I will have no peace till I find you. When will I meet you? I know that the reply to my letters is delayed, but I'm sure one day you will read them and then read them again. Perhaps you will reply. Will you?

It seems, from what Nadia wrote afterward, that the prince did not reply.

I have a lump in my throat today. I even choke on water, although everything went fine. I met the Canadian delegation and obtained the international number. I was hoping you would share this latest exile with me, or perhaps I will find you there? Nothing is impossible beyond the limits of reason because we live in a world that knows no logic. I feel tired. Can I postpone writing? Well, I will go to sleep; maybe I will see you in my dreams.

The rain gently knocked at the door. Listening to the harmony of the rain and the whirling wind, I felt as if I were listening to music coming from very distant times. But at this instant I was united with Nadia.

My prince, I have finished all the procedures. I don't know if I will have enough time to write to you from Amman. I fill my days with wishes. My future encounter with you is what preoccupies me. Sometimes I get confused and plunge into remembrance. I say to myself, "Calm down so you won't go mad," and I forget that I'm actually standing on the edge of madness, but then I feel pleasure. Don't be surprised: I feel pleasure mixed with pain. The news of the homeland arrives with the new immigrants, but it is so scarce. Despite its scarcity, it reveals many absent and concealed truths—more death, more killing, more disease, more militarization, more darkness, and more preparations for the next war. People are falling, and there is no hope. And between this pain and the pleasure of taking refuge in you, I understand the scope of the catastrophe. Did you know that my uncle died? I am sorry to tell you they killed him. When corpses were scattered during the days of the uprising and the regime took control, we were confined in our houses for three days. On the fourth day, we heard my uncle's voice calling my mother; we didn't know how he had managed to get there. When my mother opened the door, my uncle was there looking at a man's body near the threshold; he just wanted to get it out of the way. They shot him on the spot (it was forbidden to bury corpses; they said to let the dogs devour them). When my mother gasped, one of them aimed his gun at her chest, but for some reason he didn't shoot; he withdrew, saying, "Scum. You're all scum, and we'll take revenge on you." I huddled up under the stairs between neglected corpses, smelling death, and Nadir was in army training and couldn't take a day off. I don't know why I'm telling you about atrocities you have experienced yourself. Let me finish this letter because depression has descended upon me, and I don't want you to be infected.

The gusts of rain increased, accompanied by thunder and the lamenting wind, as if the whole sky were weeping and crying. Cold air crept through the gaps in the door and window. I covered myself with the blanket. I didn't care anymore about the smells it emitted. My body was used to it now. I felt warmth, not because of the blankets, but because of the love letters. This love story was mad—a madness like standing on the sharp edge of a mountain with a very steep slope. Two lovers separated by national events and then reunited on paper, but from one side only. A woman who dedicated herself to a lost lover—she would never find him—and a man, indifferent in his absence, who didn't know about the woman dedicated to his love.

> O absent-present prince, I'm putting myself together to pass into my exile. I'm hungry for you. Your face will pursue me wherever I go, for I cannot forget you. My strength to survive comes from you; perhaps I will finally tap the dregs and after that will stop traveling with you. Sometimes I feel weak from the weight of life upon me. The countdown started in Amman, and when it ends, I'll be going to settle in Canada.

Nadia didn't go to Canada, but to a tomb, without bothering to gather up her things. She didn't need a passport this time. Not even a ticket. She carried no clothing bag, no memories, no feeling of regret or satisfaction or love. Was she desperate for her prince? Did she ever erase him from her memory? Did she reach the point where she could bury her past, right before the instant separating life and death?

I put the notebook away and closed my burning eyes. The rain let up, and the wind stopped lamenting. I gave in to drowsiness. A few blurred images passed my mind's eye, and then I suddenly plunged into sleep.

WE JOSTLED AGAINST THE IRON-GATED DOOR. In the chaos, no one could hear anyone else. The officer stretched his hand through the bars, holding out papers—papers of residency, papers for new appointments, incomplete papers to be returned to their owners. From time to time, he protested against the tumult. "Attention, please! Listen to what I say! Stop all this confusion at once! The people who are here for interviews will enter first."

But the crowds refused to calm down. They were holding onto the iron bars like prisoners, yelling, complaining, desperate, furious. The officer, frustrated with their disobedience, turned his back and disappeared angrily behind interior doors. The voices died down; some people blamed each other, others just fell silent, and yet others, like volcanoes waiting to explode, suppressed their anger. The women withdrew to the sidewalk, and the men remained standing, waiting for their turn. A long time passed before the officer reappeared, and, pointing his finger, he stressed the necessity of remaining calm lest he go away and not return. A man leaning on an iron bar called to him, "Brother, please . . ."

The officer came closer to the man, who said to him imploringly, "You ought to be more patient, for them"— he pointed at the women and the children. "Their condition is miserable; you have to look at their requests in a way that acknowledges their humanity."

The officer didn't seem to comprehend what the man said. He just nodded and asked the people to form two lines, one for men and the other for women, and to keep silent so that they could hear what he was going to say. When we had complied, he began to read off numbers, asking some to enter. A few steps away stood a young man with his arms around his chest. Every time I accidentally looked around, I caught him staring at me as though he knew me.

"Huda Abdel Baqi."

"Yes?"

"Sorry. Your application is rejected." The officer handed me the application, saying, "You can appeal."

I was speechless as I took the paper. I felt as if I were sinking in quicksand and asked myself how this wide world could refuse me refuge in any one of its corners. I was about to yell, cry, rebel, but I contained myself to preserve some remnant of pride. I walked a few steps away from the Refugee Office, and the young man joined me.

"It doesn't matter; there's still a chance."

I looked at him, a young man in his thirties, tall and dark. His eyes were black, and he was rather slim. I didn't say anything. I walked toward the fence and leaned against it.

The young man began to explain without my asking. "This happens a lot when the committee is not convinced by the reports. In the case of an appeal, the demand is transferred to another committee, which reads the information anew. It happened to my brother, and he is now a refugee in Australia."

I didn't make any comment, so he asked me, "Who else is with you in your file?"

I replied with a sadness I couldn't conceal, "No one is with me. I'm on my own."

He went on, asking, "Where's your family?"

I wanted to cry, but I held back the tears. "There's only my grandmother left, and she's in Baghdad."

After some silence, he spoke again. "I'm sorry. What is your case? As you know, or perhaps you don't know, being granted refugee status depends on a clear and justified case: those who are escaping the death penalty or are fugitives from imprisonment, including those who were accused of acting against the regime or who suffered clear evidence of damage. In all cases, they need documents to prove their claims."

We walked together toward the bus stop. I told him about my problems while he explained the system to me. "The committee has to verify all information because some of the asylum seekers turn out to be sent by the regime to spy on others, either here in Amman or in their countries of settlement."

Surprised, I asked, "Is that possible? How can Iraqis spy on Iraqis under such circumstances?"

He answered painfully, "Bankruptcy, lack of prospects, and desperation overpower the good in souls, so these people become instruments to spy on their fellow citizens."

I looked at him as we waited at the bus stop. I didn't know why, but I suspected he might be one of those sent by the regime. I regretted disclosing my problems and paid no attention to what he said after that. I jumped onto the bus without saying good-bye, but his lips were moving when I looked back at him as the bus left. I had a feeling that he wanted to say something important. What could he be saying in that last moment?

A HUNDRED ANXIOUS AND HORRIFYING HOURS under the most violent bombing by the militaries of thirty countries were relived in Nadia's diary. It was hellfire, and the

Iraqis were the firewood. Intensified and blind bombing, mass flight, terrible anger, and one single question with no answer: Why did the president so obstinately continue with the invasion if he knew he was going to withdraw from Kuwait anyway? This question was on everyone's minds before and after the outbreak of the war.

On February 26, 1991, troops had headed down a wide desert road. They had returned in failure and defeat. On the road, they had been a target of the enemies' planes despite the withdrawal order, which many commanders hadn't believed, knowing the president's stubborn insistence on putting them in one hell or another. They had been returning home, frustrated. Under fire, they had melted into their vehicles' steel, and their bodies had been carbonized. The fortunate ones had walked hundreds of miles, torn with hunger and humiliation, and many had fled to the Saudi border, looking for escape.

The feeling of humiliation was shared among the army and the people, who had no hope of relief except through revolt. The first spark started in Basra and spread to the other provinces. The defenseless people were moved by despair, isolation, bitter defeat, oppression, and the widening gap between them and their ruler. This is how it was: vanquished people and angry, demoralized troops who had left behind them burned corpses and damaged machinery came together. Statistics say that thousands of troops had chosen captivity and that 65 percent had deserted from the army; ten thousand troops had fallen dead on the road in retreat.

Police stations, ministries, and party organizations fell into the insurgents' hands. Some of their occupants ran away, and others joined the uprising. The starving people broke into the government stores of grain and food and took everything they could carry. Wounded soldiers sought refuge in houses where they were not asked for their names. Names had no importance in those horrible hours. Nadia wrote in her diary how she rushed to assist the wounded. On her way back, she saw a fallen soldier near their house. At first, she didn't recognize him. She held his hands to help him stand up. His clothes were covered with blood. Then she heard him whisper, "Nadia, don't worry. This blood is not mine. I'm hungry and don't have the strength to walk."

She couldn't believe that it was Emir. His face was soiled with mud, and his eyes were hollow. He fell into her arms, almost fainting.

"Try for me, my darling. Please. Hold on."

At home, she offered him some water and wiped his face. Her mother rushed to give him some of Nadir's clothes.

"Take this, my son, and I will prepare you something to eat. As for your clothes, I will burn them."

Emir recovered after two days and joined the insurgents. The provinces fell one after the other. Emir did not return to Nadia's house. She thought that he had gone to Hiyania to reassure his family, but he never reached them. Instead, he met an officer and a sergeant from his unit. They suggested that he travel to Karbala to support the insurgents there. By the time they entered Karbala, before dawn, the holy city had already fallen into the hands of the authorities.

Everyone who has survived remembers the events of the uprising and how helicopters circled the city. Houses, factories, and stores were demolished. Armored cars entered the city, burning gardens on both sides of the street so that no one could take refuge in them. Those who attempted to escape death via the outlying roads were trapped by helicopters that poured white oil on them and then threw firebombs, reducing them to ashes. At the same time, American helicopters hovered in the skies, watching the events of the new battle of Karbala, where children were exterminated along with their mothers and the elderly. Those whom the authorities caught were transported to unknown places from which they never returned. With horror falling upon the houses, Karbala became a ghost city filled with the smells of decay. Its streets were empty except for tanks, the regime's armed men, and the bodies that no one dared to bury. The authorities had forbidden their burial so that they would serve as a warning to others. The corpses remained disfigured and rotting for many days until they were buried in unknown mass graves. The same thing happened in other districts as well. High-level officials or their friends attended execution ceremonies. On a video smuggled to many humanitarian organizations, the president's cousin Chemical Ali could be seen beating many young men to death with his shoes and the butt of his gun.

Emir vanished, like many others who died, escaped, or disappeared in secret prisons. Nadia had written in her diary, "One friend told me that Emir didn't fall into the hands of the regime, and the last time he saw Emir, Emir had said to him that he intended to return to Basra. But he never returned, and I have no news from him now."

This was how so many lost touch. Fathers didn't know anything about what had happened to their missing children and were unable to search for or ask about them. Perhaps they accepted their fate, for the missing ones never returned. Family, wives, and lovers convinced themselves that there was no way for them to meet each other again. But Nadia had kept flirting with hope, believing that Emir might have left the country, like those who succeeded in fleeing through Kurdistan or through the desert to Saudi Arabia.

EVERY TIME I went to the Refugee Office, I would see new faces. Since it was too early to let us in, the policeman at the door asked everybody to withdraw to the sidewalk. Some listened, and others grumbled. When the officer finally opened the door, everybody rushed in. I pushed my way through the crowd to hand in my appeal application. The policeman shouted, "Don't push!" A man asked about his residency permit renewal, and the officer pointed at the announcement board.

"Brothers! Please read the posted announcements. There are new instructions. There is a day for general consulting, another for residency and renewal-of-residency applications, and specific days to pick up renewals."

The man who had asked about residency said, "It is best like this."

The officer didn't reply, and others went to check the instructions on the announcement board. The women waited on the sidewalk or leaned on the fence while the officer admitted some families. I didn't know who was standing behind or next to me, and my body was becoming tense. I handed in the application and moved away with difficulty. Before I left, I noticed the young man from the other day, the one I had been suspicious about. Why did I slow down? He greeted me, and we walked together, almost as though we had prearranged it. Our steps were slow and rhythmic on the asphalt.

"Things are slow in the Refugee Office," he said. "Some will now desperately try illegal immigration. What about you?"

"I just appealed. What about you?"

"I'm accepted. I'm now waiting for an interview with the Australian delegation. I'll join my brother there. Where do you live?"

"On Mount al-Hussein. And you?"

"I live with a roommate, my friend Faisal, in al-Jandawil."

I waited for him as he bought cigarettes from one of the kiosks. He returned with two bottles of strawberry juice, and we sat on a bench. I looked at him while he was lighting up a cigarette. His face looked different, but his features were difficult to forget: mysterious black eyes, a coffee-colored complexion with the trace of a healed wound above his left eyebrow. This time his features inspired confidence, and I didn't feel suspicious about him, but I was still uncertain. I felt that he was concealing something, and this impression would be confirmed in subsequent encounters.

When the bus came, he wrote his cell phone number on a piece of paper. "If you need anything, don't hesitate to contact me."

I took the paper, looking at him as though promising him an appointment. When the bus started moving, we waved to each other, each of us hiding something confused deep inside.

EVERY TIME I dialed the number for home, I was disappointed. Baghdad preferred to keep silent, as if punishing me for having abandoned it. Every time I asked myself questions, I developed a headache. Days and months passed slowly, and I felt like a desert sojourner lost in a mirage that was failing to quench my thirst. I was unable to change the map of my exile, and I couldn't return to Baghdad.

I climbed the long stairs to my room, and before I reached it, I had to sit down on the last stair to catch my breath. Umm Ayman came out to tell me that she was about to rent my room to someone else. The carpenter from the downstairs shop needed wood storage; otherwise, he would have to find another place for his growing business. She apologized, trying to look sympathetic as she explained the situation, and said that she would give me until the end of the month to look for a decent place. While she was rambling, I thought about the burden of looking and bargaining for a new place.

At that moment, my hand felt the paper in my jacket pocket. I immediately thought of calling him; then it occurred to me that I didn't know his name and that he hadn't written it under his phone number. He hadn't asked me my name either. What would I tell him? Should I say I'm the girl from the Refugee Office? It was amazing that neither of us had asked the other for a name.

Umm Ayman continued, "You will be fine. I know a nice woman in Mount Amman; I think she has a vacant room much better than this one."

All day long I felt an emptiness inside me. I looked at Nadia's books on the table. They were inviting me to read them, but my head had become like a balloon, and I was so deprived of all energy because I forgot to have lunch.

After a while, Umm Ayman came back and gave me Samiha's address. I didn't miss the opportunity to see her the next day.

ON THE RIDE from Mount al-Hussein to Mount Amman, the bus passed through streets I hadn't seen before, filled with grocery shops, restaurants, and clothing boutiques. I didn't notice the din of the bus passengers; my head was still feeling empty. I got out at the last stop. I read the address that Umm Ayman had given me and soon found myself standing at Madam Samiha's door. When I rang the bell, a woman of indeterminate age and with severe features opened the door. She was wearing flowered cotton pajamas and a transparent blue head scarf.

"I'm Huda. Umm Ayman sent me."

She admitted me to a small salon, inviting me to take a seat as she sat facing me. Between us was a small, square wooden table with a Formica top. She spoke in a soft voice. "Welcome. Umm Ayman talked to me and gave me an idea about you." (I wondered what idea she'd given her about me.) "I just have one condition."

I looked at her inquiringly. She continued, "I need someone to help me at home, and in return I will waive the rent and will add ten dinars monthly."

I felt humiliated; I hadn't left my country to be a maid. I was going to say that I was a university graduate, but as though she read my mind, she explained with a smile, "I don't need someone to clean the house or to wash the dishes, as you might have thought; I already have a maid.

I need someone to look after my blind brother because my job takes a lot of my time."

I felt better, and I accepted immediately. How could I miss this opportunity when I was about to find myself penniless?

"Come, I'll show you your room."

From the kitchen door, we walked out to a small garden. "My name is Samiha, and my brother is Samih," she said, leading me down a narrow stone staircase. We walked past small budding plants and others from the Indian fig family and under a grape tree whose entangled branches reached out to iron trellises. After two or three yards, we came up to a green iron door.

"You'll feel comfortable with us, and I'll provide you with what you need. This is the room."

I followed her in. The room was wider than the one on Mount al-Hussein, with a large window overlooking the small garden. It was furnished with a wardrobe, a bedside table with two drawers, and a wooden bed covered by a faded but clean blanket. On the floor was a wine-colored carpet. In a corner, there was a small stove, and a hallway led to the bathroom. "This is a gift," I said to myself, for I had never lived in a better place than this.

"I forgot to mention that Friday is your day off," she added.

I didn't wait until the end of the month, the time limit that Umm Ayman had given me. I went ahead and gathered all my belongings in a big box and put my unfolded clothes in a bag. As I was packing, a leather wallet that was among Nadia's belongings fell out. I wanted to browse through it but refrained. "I have no time," I thought. "I'll look at it later on," and I buried it in the folds of my clothes.

The next day I was sleeping in another bed, tossing and turning, smelling the odors of other people who had slept there before me, the bed creaking at every move. I needed a few more nights to become used to the place.

HE WAS PERHAPS THIRTY-FIVE, elegant and pale skinned. His eyes didn't seem like those of a blind person; when you talked to him, you felt as though he were looking at you. He had been born with only four senses, and when he was six, his mother had placed him in a school for the blind. There he grew up, studied, and developed a fine taste for music, specializing in playing the lute. He had graduated with honors from the conservatory and taught at the same institute. He spoke quietly, but when he laughed, his laughter resounded through the air. He asked many questions whenever he couldn't understand something or when he wanted to know more about something. He knew the layout of his room, and he could walk to the living room without stumbling over the furniture. His clothes were always clean and elegant. That was Samih.

As for my job, I started at four o'clock in the afternoon after Samih returned from the school and took a small rest. My job was to read the newspapers for him, do some of his correspondence, and look after his library, which consisted of literature and art books and some cassettes and tapes. Samih was fond of poetry and interested in contemporary poets. Every day I would read more than one poem for him. I had needed some time to get used to the way of reading that he felt most comfortable with.

More than once he would stop me, asking me to give him some time to think so that he could absorb the meaning and capture the image in his mind. He would repeat to me that slow reading helps to charge the words with feeling and that poetry is more about feelings than about mere words. He recited many poems from memory for me, and I was amazed at his control of the language. He had a profound stillness in his voice, as though it came from the depths of history. Words flowed from between his lips as if they were living creatures. He was fond of poems by al-Sayyab, and his lute never left his side.[10]

One day Samih played for me the poem "A Stranger by the Gulf" with a melody different from the one sung by Sa'doun Jaber. While he played, I imagined al-Sayyab's pain in his exile. My tears flowed silently, hot and burning. After Samih finished playing, he said that he had never found a poem that depicted exile as al-Sayyab did in this poem. I didn't say anything for fear of betraying my emotions, but he sensed the state I had fallen into.

"You're crying."

"I remembered my family."

He put the lute aside and began talking about beautiful things hidden in our souls and how we fail to see them. "These feelings are like buried ore. We only need patience and a little drilling to find them, like those who toil for gold in the mines."

While he was talking, I was wondering about the limits of his knowledge of archaeology and relics—he

10. Badr Shakir al-Sayyab (1926–64): Iraq's most celebrated poet and one of the pioneers of the free-verse movement.

who never saw the outer face of life. Despite these limits, I felt as if he were trying to open a window for me to a world that I wasn't able to approach, the world of the innermost feelings that we usually ignore or lose sight of in life's clamor. But those feelings soon vanished at night, when my sorrows flourished and I realized that time was slipping away. Every night I tried to recollect my soul as if to reconnect it to its original womb. But anxiety roamed through my body, squeezing me and snapping at my flesh until I felt I was shrinking. Alone at night, I murmured, while memory, like a naughty child, dug up the past, uncovering the details I had buried. I lay in wait for obscure voices—voices infused with the darkness that crept under the blankets and clothes to reach my bones.

Samiha turned out to be a very kind woman. In my mind, her severe features smoothed into calmness and softness. In the mornings, she would drop Samih off at the conservatory and then go to work at one of the banking companies. She would insist that I eat breakfast with them, and on holidays she would invite me to lunch. From time to time, she would ask me about my situation in Amman and about my family back in Baghdad. We would often find ourselves drawn into conversations about politics, and I found out her bold and frank opinions about the miserable reality of the Arab world. Within a short period, she was able to break through my psychological reserve toward strangers; I felt so comfortable that I confessed my problems. She was very sympathetic and told me, "The place is yours; you're safe here—and don't hesitate to ask for anything." I was almost in tears from the emotions that this fine woman stirred in me. Later on I would learn that she'd dedicated her life to her brother and had never married. On another occasion, she would confess to me that she'd had a single love affair and that at the end of it she had closed the door on her feelings.

WE GATHERED EARLY in front of the Refugee Office. As usual, some women sat on the sidewalk. Through the bars, we stared at the courtyard. I was looking at the newcomers, but I was also looking for a black-eyed young man with a dark complexion and a well-proportioned body. I didn't find him.

A cold wind played with the branches, and the rain drizzled onto faces and sidewalks. The officer appeared with a bundle of papers, and everybody stretched their hands out and clung to the bars, getting ready to go in. He handed out a few small numbered cards, letting in those with numbers up to fifty. Since it was the consulting day, I asked about my case.

"Nothing for you for now," he said. "Give us a call if you cannot come."

I began scanning the faces again, looking for the brown-faced man. Something told me he wasn't coming that day, but his shadow walked with me to the bus stop, accompanied me on the ride home, and bade me farewell at my door. I couldn't breathe as I sat alone, thinking about my status. It occurred to me to contact him. I looked for his phone number in my purse pocket and walked out to the closest phone booth.

I think he had been asleep, for his voice was soft and hoarse. "Yes? Who is it?"

"It's me. Sorry. I'm the girl that you met at the Refugee Office."

I imagined him getting up from his bed.

"I'm glad you called. Where are you?"

"I didn't see you today at the Refugee Office."

"I was there yesterday and met with the Australian delegation."

"Congratulations."

"It hasn't been finalized yet. The process is long, and this interview doesn't mean final acceptance."

"I hope that what happened to me never happens to you."

"No, I've been officially accepted as a refugee; if Australia refuses me, I'll simply be transferred to another country. And what did they tell you?"

"They haven't decided yet."

"Listen, I want to see you—that is, if you want to see me, of course."

I said hastily, "Of course I do. I need some help understanding a few things."

"So let's meet tomorrow morning at ten in front of the Roman Theatre in Hashemite Square."

We ended our conversation at that point, and we had still forgotten to ask for each other's name.

WHY WAS I GOING TO SEE THIS OTHER MAN? Did I need someone to support my soul, inspire patience in me, and protect me from shattering loss? Or did I need a stick to guide my steps along the unknown road and its obscure twists and turns? I repeated these questions hundreds of times during the night. I was filled with sorrow. Darkness besieged, ambushed me, wresting me from sleep, and I felt helplessly off balance. I asked myself what I was looking for. The wind blew at my door, shaking it violently and filling me with anxiety. Defenseless, I fought off thousands of fingers, peeling them away from my throat, only to have them grab my neck once again. I severed them from my neck, only to feel them approaching my heart, playing with its pulse, leading me to the brink of the precipice.

That will be my constant state in exile, especially if I can't find anybody to whom I can express my sorrow.

Are you sure?

Not completely.

What do you want exactly?

Perhaps I need a man whose fingers will warm me up and pull out the roots of my exile.

Which man?

I don't know.

Here you are. You don't know, and in order to know you have to watch your step.

I was confused and agitated as I went to meet him. There was nothing tying us together except exile. On my way to Hashemite Square, I rearranged words in my mind. I hesitated and stopped halfway. I knew I had to rein in my horse before it bolted.

You aren't the type whose horse will bolt.

Is this a compliment or an insult?

Choose whichever fits you.

I don't know which one fits me.

I arrived at Hashemite Square, and there he was, waving; I walked toward him with confused feelings. I sat in front of him in one of the cafés. I felt safe and at the same time cautious—safe because he was a fellow countryman carrying the odors of the two muddy rivers, but cautious because something still unknown was digging into my soul. Perhaps my confusion came from my natural lack of confidence, thanks to my grandmother's constant advice: "Beware of men; don't trust them. Take and don't give. Hold the stick from the middle. Don't lean too far to either end; otherwise, you'll be lost. Take your time before you announce anything so that the man doesn't feel as if you have thrust yourself upon him."

Grandma, I haven't taken anything, and I haven't given either. I've learned not to trust quickly, as you advised; my relationship with Youssef took a long time to form, even though he was my cousin. It grew gradually, with no place for passion; meanwhile, my soul was longing for an indomitable burning love, a tempestuous love like those I read about in novels. My meetings with Youssef were unadventurous. They were permitted because of our kinship and thus had become ordinary. And although that relationship didn't resemble those in my dreams, I held on to it, clinging to its threads. It was falling apart now, while I was thousands of miles away, as if our time together hadn't tightened our bond as much as I or we had hoped. Was it the war and the long years of military service that had carried him to death's threshold? Or was the nation's destruction over the past thirty years ruining intimate relationships, love, happiness, and personal contentment? Yet Nadia had also loved at the same time and under the same circumstances. She had also been in exile and had suffered perhaps more than I did, yet here were her love letters despite the fact that she didn't know what had happened to her lover. What was the difference? Did I have a heart of stone? I didn't know how to explain or categorize my feelings. Sometimes it seemed as if I were waiting for a man I still didn't know and that he would not come. Sometimes I would long for

Youssef, and sometimes I would feel free of any obliga-
tion to him. But he still remained the first man in my
life. So why did I walk toward the other one? What type
of relationship would bind me to a man whose name I
didn't even know? Was my story with Youssef over?

The waiter put two Cokes and two glasses on the
table between us. I fidgeted, feeling doubtful as I stole
a glance at him. But that feeling vanished as soon as he
spoke because I had curbed the suspicion I felt at our first
meeting. Perhaps I was merely embarrassed.

"What's wrong?"

"I don't know."

"We are in a public place."

"I know that."

"And we are foreigners here; no one is observing us
or counting our breaths."

I didn't reply to this.

"Your voice is distinctive on the phone."

"And now?"

"It is still distinctive. But when we don't see things,
we feel them more, which means we can see things with
our feelings."

The image of Samih fell between us but quickly
disappeared.

"Are we going to speak like strangers?"

"You're right."

"My name is Moosa Kadhim. And you?"

"Huda. Huda Abdel Baqi."

"You give the impression of calmness at first."

"Then?"

"There is a sleeping volcano behind your appearance,
which might explode at any time."

His assessment was right. Although I seemed calm and even submissive, something was churning inside, to the point that I sometimes felt like a wild cat who wanted to bite everything and would devour herself when she couldn't. I could have turned into a furious tiger, but my fury couldn't find a way out. It was suppressed inside my soul, burning my nerves at night as I tossed and turned.

"We're all dying volcanoes," I said to Moosa. "I'm hoping I find a refuge to keep me from erupting and burning up. Tell me, what should I do if they reject my appeal?"

He opened a Coke can and poured some in my glass. The foam spilled over.

"Give it some time. Why are you so nervous?"

"What if they reject me?"

He opened the other can and poured some Coke in his glass.

"The reason why you felt you needed to leave Iraq was based on a little exaggeration by the regime's people. There are no secret inks, no modern machines, and no handwriting experts to trap you. They circulated this information to scare people."

"What has happened, happened. I'm not here to analyze what I left behind. I'm in trouble, and I have no one to turn to."

He lit a cigarette and began to smoke. Then, as if lifting a weight from his chest, he said, "If you want, we can make a deal."

I was taken aback, and my heart sank. I prepared myself for the unknown. I looked into his deep eyes, searching for the answers.

"We can get married so that your name can be added to my file and you can be safe here. Then you can emigrate with me to the new country."

I had never expected such a thing. When he said "a deal," I had thought he wanted a bribe, like many others would have. I shivered, perhaps from surprise or perhaps because of the chilly wind that was agitating everything around us.

After I absorbed what he said, and we exchanged glances, I said, "If you want an immediate answer, I have nothing to say."

He slowly inhaled his cigarette and said, "Of course, you'll need some time to make a decision. Think about it and feel completely free to accept or reject the offer."

I couldn't sleep that night. I kept hearing unknown species of insects buzzing. The wind blew through the tree branches. The door's groaning harmonized with my soul's moaning. I looked at all sides of the situation. At first, I felt neutral, then I felt confused, but later on I began to lean toward the idea. Moosa was still a mystery to me, though. I wasn't in love with him, for my heart was still attached to Youssef. And even if I had been free of feelings for Youssef, I wouldn't be able to fall in love just for the sake of a dubious bargain that came at the wrong time and in the wrong place. I felt split into two persons: one wanted an unknown adventure, and the other was holding back; one asked questions, and the other answered them as she shrank inside her cocoon:

Do you deny that you approached him?

Perhaps because I needed companionship.

That is the beginning of a love relationship.

My heart is still guarded.

Don't hide behind transparent veils; you have no choice, no other escape.

Perhaps there is light at the end of the tunnel. Perhaps Youssef will show up.

Remember, here you are a woman in exile from the Land of Holy Men, and tunnels might lead to other, darker, tunnels.

But I don't know him.

You'll get to know him. In the beginning, men are like locked trunks, and only women who wish to can have the keys.

I want a man I can love, not marry.

You won't find the love you want, so embark with the first captain you encounter in exile.

Every time I felt sleepy, a thorn would pierce me into alertness. *Moosa, are you the captain who will lead my lost ship to the safety of land? Or are you just a piece of driftwood that I will hold onto in a stormy sea that will soon engulf me?* I knew that the piece of wood would not save me from drowning, yet I would eventually reach out to it, just not this quickly. Yes, I will announce my consent to his proposal because perhaps the piece of wood will turn out to be a skiff that will save me from sinking. My grandmother would say, "In front of the man you want, pretend to be hesitant; that will earn you respect and put you in a high position in his heart." *And you, Moosa, do you love me? Or do you just think of helping me out? And if it is love, why do you call it a "deal"? Why don't you declare it or hint at it?*

When Moosa had presented his proposal, he hadn't been persistent or obstinate. As soon as he had made the offer, he had moved on to another subject; he had begun to talk about himself.

"When I arrived in Amman, I worked in a restaurant and then in a bakery while receiving help from my brother in Australia. I had encountered hardships in the refugee camps and during my flight to Iran after the failed uprising."

He had taken two puffs of his cigarette and continued. "My life is a chain of failures for which I am not responsible. In my childhood, my mother died of electrocution. My father remained faithful to her memory and did not take another wife. I wished he had because my two brothers and I could have escaped his holding his 'great sacrifice' over our heads every time we wanted to choose a different path than what he wanted in life. And in my first youth, I loved our neighbor's daughter, but I was too shy to tell her; I was surprised—after more than a year of silent love—when she married a wealthy man, although she had known about my feelings. Perhaps she had become tired of my silence. Anyway, it was a teenage love. Fate played a game to deprive me of ever enjoying my true love, for it was born during times of war, trenches, fierce battles, death, and loss."

Moosa had spoken about his life with pain and sarcasm. But he would soon dispense with both as though he wanted to be done with his memories. In an attempt to give the present an importance it didn't deserve, he'd said, "I don't hold on to the past much because the present is more worthy of interest."

Despite this statement, Moosa hadn't seemed optimistic. I felt that he had contradicted himself. My relationship with him didn't seem to be anything more than a temporary friendship dictated by the circumstances of exile. Otherwise, how could I explain the longing I still felt for Youssef?

"You have to think seriously about the present," he'd continued. "I assure you that together we will wipe out these days' wounds."

I felt so grateful to this man who was offering to give me his name, but I still wasn't sure he was going to give me his heart. I thought about this for a long time, and for many nights I slept only with confusion between acceptance and refusal. Deep inside me came a cry that I was betraying Youssef. This painful feeling smothered me, but in an attempt to assuage my anxiety I would assure myself that I hadn't decided yet. I wrestled with the decision in my heart, the two choices changing places every other instant.

I cried out with a voice that was merely a whisper in my bones, "Youssef, Youssef. Nothing comes from you, and nothing goes to you. Where do you stand? I'm getting more and more confused."

I was desperately trying to get in touch with Youssef, but the phone line was always silent. I felt worn out from my days in Amman, as if slow death and moral disintegration had clung to me since my flight here. I'd been looking for guidance, but I had lost it. What was this blind wandering I had fallen into?

SAMIH SUGGESTED that we sit on the balcony. The weather was warm, and the morning wind was mild. I wondered what difference it made whether he sat on the balcony, in the room, or in any other place when he couldn't see. The large balcony overlooked the foot of a mountain covered with red- and green-tiled roofs.

Twisted streets crossed the area, and rows of pine trees and cypress surrounded some of the buildings. We sat on a bamboo couch. He surprised me when he asked, "Isn't the landscape beautiful from this angle?" I needed a few seconds to recover from my surprise before I answered, "Yes, it is really beautiful." I wondered how the blind could locate or even recognize beauty.

I was sitting at the other end of the couch, a pile of newspapers and books between us that Samiha had put there before she left. Samih's listening rituals required that I read the newspaper headlines out loud, and if a title sounded interesting, I would then read the details for him. When I read literary materials, he would remind me to read slowly so that he could capture the image in his imagination.

Fianca, a maid from Sri Lanka, put two cups of coffee on the table. I offered Samih a cup, and our fingers touched. This type of contact often happens unintentionally, but on that day I felt that he did it on purpose. I ignored what happened, and I began reading newspaper headlines and titles for him, but he didn't stop me to pursue the details. I had the feeling he was distracted, with no desire to listen. After I finished, he grabbed his lute and started tuning it.

He asked, "Do you like music?"

I replied unenthusiastically, "Certainly not as much as you do. I was born in a time when music was considered vanity, and now we've lost the capacity for the meditation needed to enjoy music."

Then he asked, "And what else?"

"Our life is so noisy with—drums, madness, cries, and songs of past and future wars."

"What about poetry? Aren't you from the country of poetry and poets?"

"We still celebrate what al-Mutanabbi said and what our ancestors left.[11] But now we have only two types of poems: the first glorifies idols and wars, and the second narrates the defeat of men and the horrors of those calamities. The second type is written outside the country. The era of celebration, music, and poetry is gone, and great artists have gone into exile and begun to write their sorrows from afar. Do you want me to tell you some of what Dunya Mikhail said?"

I explained to him that Dunya Mikhail is a poet from the wartime generation. His fingers fell away from the strings as he listened to "The War Works Hard."

> *How diligent the war is,*
> *How eager and efficient*
> *Early in the morning*
> *It wakes up the sirens*
> *it dispatches ambulances to different places*
> *Swings corpses into the air*
> *Glides stretchers to the wounded*
> *Summons rain from mothers' eyes*
> *Digs into the earth, extracting many things from under the*
> *   rubble*
> *Rigid and glittering things and others faded that still pulse*
> *Entertains the gods*
> *By shooting fireworks and missiles*

11. Abou-t-Tayyib Ahmad ibn al-Husayn al-Mutanabbi: an Arab (Iraqi-born) poet regarded as one of the greatest poets in the Arabic language.

Into the sky
Plants mines in the fields
Urges families into exile
War continues its work day and night
Inspires tyrants to throw off long speeches
Bestows medals on generals, and themes for poets
It contributes to the industry of artificial limbs
Provides food for flies
Adds pages to the history books
Achieves equality between killer and killed
Teaches lovers how to write letters
Trains young girls to waiting
Fills newspapers with stories and pictures
Builds places for orphans
Enlivens the industry of coffin makers
Pats grave diggers on the shoulder
Draws smiles on the faces of leaders
Indeed, it works really hard
Yet no one praises it with a single word.

I looked at him. His face was quiet, as if in another world.

I asked, "Are you with me?"

He answered, "Of course. I'm meditating on the poem."

I wanted to ask how he "saw" things around him: the people, the trees, the colors, but I was afraid of offending him. Then he said, "How sorry I feel for what is happening in Iraq."

I didn't comment, and a thick silence fell between us. The lute was still in his hands, but he put it aside, saying, "I have no desire to play."

I guess he didn't want to increase my sorrow. He started talking about a man he had heard about on television who was living with 250 poisonous vipers and another man who was sleeping with six tigers. I asked myself what this had to do with me.

I said, "How can a person do that?"

He attributed it to man's ambition to know the hidden secrets of the human soul and said that as long as there is a will, man will be able to domesticate the most savage animals.

"But the instinct of fear often dominates man," I objected.

He said, "Sometimes fear is acquired, but, regardless, if man overcomes the fear inside him, he will be able to accomplish marvels. Fear is the first stumbling block, and if man dominates it, the route becomes easier, however difficult it might look."

He took his own case as an example, as if to answer the question I had wanted to ask.

"I was born blind. I do not know the details of faces or colors. What's red, and what does 'blue' mean? How is the day or the night? What do the sea, the sky, and the stars look like? I see them with my heart. You see with sunlight during daytime, and lamps illuminate your nights; I see things through my own inner light, which is difficult to explain to you."

While he was talking, I was wondering how and in what colors he dreamed. But, as before, I left the question unasked; perhaps he would talk about it.

He leaned back and continued. "Smells play an important role in knowing things around me, as well as sounds and touch. These senses are stronger for blind people than they are for the rest of you, who are really occupied with colors, masses, and things you see. This occupation weakens the senses because those with sight focus only on the exterior and neglect the inside, which requires contemplation and a desire to discover. You, for example . . ."

I had been gazing at a flock of birds soaring and dipping, but I listened closer to him as he said, "I sense that you are a beautiful woman. I don't know what you look like, but I see you with my 'insight.' Your depths speak to me. This is not flattery. Before I met you, I had encountered more than one woman at work and social occasions. My music professor a few years ago didn't make me feel she was beautiful, but I could feel the beauty of the professor of musical aesthetics."

He clapped his hands as though putting an end to the conversation. "I hope that what I said is clear; I hope that you'll give yourself the opportunity to rid your voice of its sadness and that you'll discover the beauty inside you."

BY THIS TIME, I should have reached a clear decision about my relationship with Moosa. If my refugee appeal was rejected, there would be no other options available. But what Moosa offered was not to be taken lightly. It was an engagement in an adopted country to someone whose character I couldn't even guess at. What unknown ramifications would there be? I hadn't discussed these details with him or even with myself. I also didn't know if my marriage with him would be a formality that would end as soon as its purpose was served. Or had I moved something inside Moosa that made him propose?

What could I do with my shaking heart every time I remembered Youssef? What about my feelings for this man with whom my life had blossomed? Despite his absence, his eyes accused me, looking at me suspiciously every time I got closer to Moosa. Did I love Moosa, or did I just like in him the man I was missing? Which man did I want? Every time I came close to decision, I would get confused again. My memories of Youssef covered a stretch of long years, but where was he now? My view of Moosa was unclear and agitated. I was connected to Youssef by a painful past full of waiting, love, and hope—framed completely by a time of bitter war. But there was nothing connecting me to Moosa. If only someone would answer the phone in Baghdad; if only I knew what had happened to Youssef.

Six months had passed since I had last talked to him. Even Youssef's friend Hani didn't know anything about him; he said he had sent Youssef a letter desperately trying to get in touch with him but hadn't received any reply. My life was poised on a delicate balance; I didn't know when I would be tipped off or where I would be when I fell. My head was spinning, and my body surrendered to torpor. It was past midnight, and I was snatching at foggy visions but eventually fell asleep.

Nadia entered my room, alighting like an angel with two blue wings. She stood at the door and looked into every corner. She seemed wretched and annoyed. She extended a hand with golden fingers, grabbed her notebook off the table, and started tearing it into pieces. In seconds, it became floating particles, falling like dusty snow on a freezing day. Then she disappeared behind a thick fog—I didn't know how it had entered the room.

When I woke up, I wondered what this dream meant. Why had she torn her memories? And why had she been so sad and vexed? I then remembered that I hadn't read her notebook for a long time. The morning light crept into the room, and Nadia's annoyed face pursued me all day long, but it didn't prevent me from making my way into those letters filled with impossible love.

Who will convey my letters to you? I'm getting ready to travel. They say that the world has become a village; how then can I explain this burning feeling of separation? And why does the world oppress my heartbeat and cast it outside its borders? I shouldn't believe that the world is within my hands' reach. It is huge, suspicious, and ambiguous, and it never stops separating me from you. Why should irrelevant faces repeat themselves to me, while yours remains scarce? No one conveys my letters to you, but I strive to write them anyway; perhaps by chance they will find their way to you. Despite this distance, your features are still pure and clear to me. Thinking of you makes you wholly present to me, as though we had never separated. Am I also present to you even though I am absent? There are many things I want to confess, my prince. Things are weighing on my chest and growing heavier, but they can't extinguish the passion of my flame. It still glows even as other burning candles of my life go out, dripping and flaring. You are mine. I'm sure about this. But I'm afraid I won't be yours after all this separation. What will I do with my heart then? I'm no longer a queen, as you used to call me. I'm only a wandering soul that doesn't know when it will find its way back to you.

And in another letter:

My Emir . . . Despair crept into my soul during my feverish search for you. In a cursed irrational moment, I thought about giving you up. Imagine! I gathered your letters and decided to burn them. That was before I left the country. I stood next to my mother's oven, which hadn't been heated since her death. I put in a heap of wood, poured a little oil on it, and lit it so that it glowed. I extended my hands to grab the pile of letters, but before I threw it into the blue flames, something pulled me back. Was it you standing behind me? I'm completely in love with you, my prince.

When I first set foot in Amman, for a while I breathed in a strange scent. I immediately told myself that it was the smell of freedom and deliverance, but after a few moments I discovered it was your scent. Perhaps I was deluding myself. Anyway, I convinced myself that I was going to find you here. Basra had separated us, but Amman would bring us together. What a false hope! Days, months, and years have passed by; only a few days until I leave for Canada. Right now I feel overcome by despair. Amman hasn't been kind to me, but Canada will be the same. Despair transforms me into pieces of ember and ashes, but I will stay strong. I have to resist until I see you.

Suddenly, I felt as though something had touched me, and I was shaken. I looked around, sweeping the corners of the room, and remembered my dream. It was as though a ghost were sharing the place with me. I set the notebook aside and sought refuge in God. I began thinking about many things—meeting Moosa, calling Baghdad, the Iraqi crowds at the Refugee Office. I saw Abou al-Abd calling out file numbers and Youssef's face. But I was having difficulty picturing him, as if he didn't want to be evoked. Youssef? Have you forgotten me, or do you prefer the hell inside our country? Are you satisfied with what you did when you got me the passport? Are you still waiting for new wars to come? When does your war start, my dear? What will you do if they find out that you played a role in getting me the false passport? Our last meeting was confused, and now I see you in my confused imagination. What's happening inside this room? Breathing and whispering. A heavy weight fell onto my chest, and fear pushed me outside.

It was a lovely day. White clouds with golden edges embroidered the sky. The clean streets were lively with movement. I dialed the number at a nearby phone booth, but, as before, no one answered. I walked to the newsstands and read the newspaper headlines, thought about Amman's bookstore, but I already had reading materials in Samih's library—and Nadia's books still locked in their secrets. I headed to the vegetable market and bought bread, cucumbers, and red radishes. As I was crossing Saladin Avenue to Shabsugh Street, I came face-to-face with Hani. We looked at each other for a while as though searching for names.

"Hani, I'm Huda, a relative of Youssef. Do you remember me?"

"Of course I do. How are you? We haven't heard from you."

"I was busy. I've asked about you twice and was told you had returned to Naplouse."

"But I returned two months ago."

"Tell me, have you heard from Youssef?"

"No. I tried to call him twice, but with no luck."

"I've tried many times. I don't know what's happened. I'm very worried."

"Don't be. Tomorrow morning I'm heading to Baghdad to deliver my brother Hussam's application so he can study medicine there. Do you need anything from there?"

"Thank God I met you today then! I'd like to put my mind at ease about my family and their situation. Tell Youssef to write a very detailed letter. Ask him why he's delayed his arrival in Amman. How long will you be there?"

"A week or ten days."

Those ten days took forever, as though the clock had stopped. But then it also seemed as if a flood of days came and went . . . day and night . . . night and day. My throat was bitter, and so was my bread. The hours were like rocks. Stories upon stories sprang from my head . . . shining memories . . . different faces, streets, and roads . . . houses and markets . . . A vehement longing would sweep me away as though I were floating into the air, passing over the checkpoints and then falling from the sky into Baghdad, crying with a full voice, "I'm back! Open the doors!"

But I would never go back. A pain-filled voice came as if from the depths of my throat: I will never return.

Two days after Hani left, I paid a visit to his mother, then again in another five days. Between Hani's departure and his return, my imagination hid behind hope's veils, which had often lit my way, only to fall away time and again, plunging me back into the darkness of this endless tunnel. My days were filled with thoughts of the possibilities and the impossibilities; I withered until the day Hani's mother informed me that Hani had come back at dawn. I could see him at four that afternoon, after he'd rested from the difficult journey from Baghdad to Amman.

I was agitated, alternating between hope and despair, fear of the known and the unknown, happiness and sadness. This was how I waited until I could see Hani.

"Youssef is fine. The phone numbers changed a long time ago." He pulled an envelope from his pocket. "This is a letter he sent you."

He gave me the letter, and my fingers shook as I touched it. I would have left immediately if doing so weren't rude. A shiver ran through my body, but I managed to control it. Hani took two hundred dollars from his wallet and handed it to me, saying, "It's from your grandmother. Your house is still being rented."

I drank the coffee that Hani's mother offered me as we exchanged small talk and compliments; then I excused myself and left.

The cold air played with my hair on the street. I threw my body onto the bus's seat as if doing so would shake the unseen accumulated dust from it. I didn't know how I felt as I opened my bag many times to make sure that the letter was still inside. The time stretched on and on, and the traffic signals played with my nerves; whenever the bus approached an intersection, the light turned a red that resembled war's blood and death. I eventually got off the bus and ran as though someone were chasing me. In my room, I opened the letter.

My dearest Huda,

What you should know is that I didn't deceive you, but rather that I did the impossible, so that you'll remember me as your savior and liberator. I carry your memory like a gentle breeze that greets me in the heat of the unceasing wars and bullets. Everything, my dear, has changed in us; as we have put up with miserable conditions, even our feelings have suffered from the virus of indifference. Memories can no longer rekindle our passion when its flame dies. Memories have become a toy we use to flirt with the present out of fear of the future, but it's a destructive game. Huda, I know staying in Baghdad is hard, but exile will be even more difficult. I'm a man who deluded himself that his roots were shallow and could be easily pulled out so that he could be transplanted somewhere else. But this illusion has vanished, and I have discovered that my roots run deep into the earth. They plunge into it, and it grips my feet. For this reason and after much thinking, I have found that resistance within the homeland is more likely to change the situation. I hope that you'll enjoy your life as much as you can. Right now I have no phone; I'll try to reach you through Hani. Perhaps things will change, and then our life paths might change too. My mother and your grandmother say hello to you.

Youssef

Youssef's peaceful and quiet face shone in my mind. Then it was suddenly severe; his gentle eyes became like those of a wildcat stalking a victim. My fingers began squeezing the letter as my spinning head replayed the written words. Youssef hadn't written "my love," but "dearest" and "dear." How the heart can change! It was strange that I wasn't crying, but disappointment filled my soul. Life had changed indeed, and the heart was no longer the center of affection. Hani told me what Youssef hadn't written in case the letter was opened at the checkpoints:

"Things are very bad in Iraq, and people are on the rim of a volcano. The regime will fall, and you will return."

Youssef was keeping me in limbo, waiting for the uncertain fall of the regime, and he had opened the door for me to go to the other man. I found myself answering Youssef's letter with words that my heart couldn't utter.

Dear Youssef,

From now on, I have to look for some blank pages where I can record a new memory of the coming days without you. You are cutting the thread that might have brought us together again. I'll also need a skin that never knew the blows of separation. I yearn for a new song away from old streams and plaintive southern melodies. I'll try to embark to the ports of oblivion before I drown in the sea of remembrance. Only now do I realize that the distance between us is wide and impossible. Don't worry, I'll find another place where I can write down lighter memories for a heart torn by exile. I pledge that I won't fall in love because that's a frightening, difficult thing.

I didn't record this letter on paper; I let it loose to float in my thoughts so that I could make it forgettable. I "read" it many times and realized that I was actually writing it for myself, urging myself to take a stand. I began an internal dialogue, finding excuses and justifications for Youssef; it didn't matter if the dialogue was naive, tense, and fragmentary, as long as it could lead to acceptance of reality.

I remembered the last scene we had together. Youssef, you didn't even give me a chance to bid you a proper farewell; it was as though you were escaping from me. Were you really avoiding me? Was it you who disappointed my heart, or was it my heart that disappointed you? Did I have to go through all this to know that feelings change like seasons? Or was the notion that Huda was for Youssef and Youssef for Huda just an illusion nurtured by our kinship and our families' hints? Did we believe the story, or did we just agree to play along? Let's admit, my dear, while great distances separate us, that we were not qualified enough for love, or perhaps I was not qualified to play the heroine's role in your life. In any case, you are excused, as you cut off your dreams before they can turn into nightmares.

After that, although Youssef still occupied my room's walls and corners, infiltrating my bed, stealing my sleep, he could appear only like a furtive image, and when he tried to stay longer, he would flicker and disappear.

Two days later I accidentally encountered Moosa at the Refugee Office. He cast a glance full of reproach at me. But before he could utter a word, I began defensively explaining my preoccupation, as though driving away the accusation that I had been avoiding him. What bound me to him and made me look for excuses? And why did I become defensive?

As we entered the Refugee Office, he remained silent. We chose a corner away from the noise and smoke filling the room. He told me then that he had completed the medical clearance (the most important step), and he was there to find out a few things related to his case.

At that moment, Abou al-Abd appeared, calling, "2426."

"Yes?"

"Please, madam."

The residency officer told me that after careful reexamination, the committee had accepted my request. When I came out, Moosa was waiting for me and congratulated me even before I told him the news. My eyes were unable to hide my happiness. Then Moosa was called, and he went into one of the rooms.

I was filled with joy, agitation, sadness—a desire to run, fly, escape. People were staring at me, and I realized that I was pacing rapidly back and forth. When I noticed what I was doing, I walked outside and sat under the shadow of one of the trees until Moosa came out. He suggested that we go to one of the cafés. I agreed, and a blissful feeling welled up in me, as though I had just woken up from a nightmare. As we talked, I scanned his face to see how he was reacting to my news. I wondered if he had wished for the opposite of this result. I noticed that he was sad and disappointed. His eyes were dull, although they had been sparkling only a half hour ago.

"What's wrong?" I asked him, although I knew the answer.

"I'm thinking about our relationship."

"What about it?"

"It's between ebb and flow. But I think things will clear up after today."

"What do you think is going to happen?"

"From the beginning, I left it up to you to choose. It is true you hadn't yet come to a decision, but this is best because if you had said yes immediately, I would have thought that I was a mere bridge to your goals. Now the situation is different."

"I think the same way. A relationship between two people has to come from the inside and not from the circumstances surrounding them. I'm really grateful to you because you tried to help me."

"And now?"

"I need some time to know the nature of my feelings."

"Over the past few days, I've been thinking a lot about you, and I understand my feelings."

"Don't you also want to give me the opportunity to understand mine? I'm going through a difficult time right now."

"What's going on?"

"A dear friend just died in Baghdad."

"Very well, I won't put pressure on you. Understand that I'll be your friend even if you refuse, and don't hesitate to ask if you need anything."

"I'm sure about that. But I need something else."

"What is it?"

I wanted to tell him that I needed to put my head on his shoulders and cry into his hands, so that his fingers would gather my tears and run through my hair. Instead, I said, "I don't know exactly. Sometimes you seem a mystery to me. I wish to know everything about you before I go ahead and marry you."

He smiled and said, "Do I really look mysterious? Although I know nothing about you, I see you clearly, and I'm sad you don't see me in the same way. I have nothing to hide except the past."

"So we need some time."

"With wars, siege, and exile, we have lost a lot of time already. We have to hold tight to what is left in our small lifetime lest it slip through our fingers."

"I need to get rid of a few things from the past."

"I'm afraid they'll say it's time for me to go. It's because of that that we don't have much time left."

"Give me one week."

"I'll wait for your answer."

He looked at me as though searching for something he had lost.

HE WAS RIGHT, but I was worried and scared. There was something standing between him and me that was preventing my feelings toward him from growing and keeping me from thinking seriously about my chances as a woman. I considered the idea of living in a strange country that I hadn't chosen for myself, and my happiness disappeared. When I put my head on the pillow, I could see the naked women, effeminate men, and Mafiosi that we had seen in their movies. I could see the apartment where I would live a lonely life between walls that would be clean yet empty of life. I would also have to master these people's language, accept their traditions, and get used to the taste of strange food. To live in a foreign country is to tear out your roots, change your lifestyle and your habits, to become familiar with skyscrapers and the mystery of forests. You have to reconsider your affections and undo the threads of your deepest commitments. It means you have to change your skin. When you finally realize all that, your country will seem like a dream that you had on a stormy night and left only a foggy vision. Would Iraq become a mere dream that had flitted through my mind? Or would my memory of it be reshaped in the new country? Would my grandmother's and Youssef's faces vanish, and would the Tigris look like a mere blue line on a world map, crossing a homeland drawn on faded paper? And would my memory slowly fade so that houses, shops, cafés, shrines, and mosques would end up as infinitely small, almost untouchable dots—or would they all remain large, clear, and sharp inside my soul? This was why I should be with a man from my own country—it would bring me back to balance; otherwise, an obscure future awaited me. My eyes were still shut as the last of these images crossed my mind. When I got up, I found that I was still trying to reach a decision.

THE RAIN that had been pouring down since early morning forced me to stay in my room. I spent the hours of the day reading from a collection of Fawzi Kareem's poems and browsing day-old newspapers. At four that afternoon, my daily duties began.

Attached to Samih's room was a smaller room where we would sit when the weather was too cold for the balcony. Everything in this room had an Arabian style—handmade carpets on the floor and paintings of desert landscapes with waving dunes, caravans of camels and running horses decorating the walls. In the middle of the room, there was a fireplace in which the glowing coals and ashes were actually made out of metal, illuminated from the inside by an electric lamp. On another wall were shelves filled with pitchers, silver bibelots, and small statues of bronze and ivory. Samiha and I exchanged the usual greetings. Samih was already in the room when I went in. We drank the coffee that Fianca had prepared. Samiha came in and handed me some wrapped-up newspapers, excused herself, and left.

I was tired and depressed. After a few minutes, Samih said, "You are not with me. You have a problem."

I wanted to cry but held on to what remained of my will to contain myself. It was amazing how Samih had such a sharp feeling for things. I envied him.

"How do you know?"

"It is clear from the tone of your voice. If you don't mind, tell me about your worries."

"Being far away from my family is painful, and this exile is killing me."

"The worst is when we feel estranged among our own people."

"Have you known exile?"

"Well, a blind person is an alien, a stranger to his environment. But in truth I'm in harmony with myself, and that's what makes me look at things from a different angle. If I could have seen and looked at the emotional reactions of sadness, joy, and fear, maybe I would have suffered much more. But feelings reliably showed me the human condition in a different way, and I know the tones of voices even if I haven't seen their owners for a long time. This is how I can recall my mother's voice even though she passed away ten years ago, and I feel a longing for the people I know whenever I haven't seen them for a while: longing but not loneliness."

"Don't you think longing and loneliness are inseparable?"

"Not always. You might feel lonely when you're around strangers, but you won't be swept toward longing as a compensation for your loneliness; alternatively, you might encounter longing for your people and your country but still be happy and contented in the place where you live."

"They are inseparable for me."

"That's because you are unhappy and discontented in your current situation."

"Can you imagine? I was burning for relocation, and now I feel as though I'm going to be uprooted; that's why I feel depressed."

"In that case, I'll give you a pass on reading poetry in particular today."

"No, reading poetry is another issue."

"On the contrary. If you are not at peace with yourself, you won't be able to express the meaning of what you read."

"I don't think about being at peace or not when I read, and, honestly, poetry itself helps me to overcome my moods, even if only temporarily."

"Okay, let's get started with poetry; then I'll play a new melody."

DESPITE THE NAGGING CONTRADICTORY IMAGES floating through my mind, I fell into a deep sleep that night from which I awoke horrified. In my dream, I had seen Nadia searching through my things; she'd pulled out her notebook, then stood in front of me and ripped it up, just like the last time, but this time she had been without her two wings. And before exiting, she had thrown an angry look at me, leaving behind tiny shreds of paper that flew and floated in the room's emptiness. These shreds had transformed into a chain of steel that had fallen to the ground, making a loud sound like a woman's scream.

I was in a panic when I awoke. I thought that I had had this nightmare because I was reading her diary, which was an assault on her personal life and perhaps would do harm to her soul. But what should I do with the diary? Should I avoid it? Tear it up? Or take it to the cemetery and bury it near her head? My throat was dry, and my bones were trembling. What was torturing Nadia's soul? How could I reach it? And how could I prevent these dreams and nightmares? I shouldn't have read her secrets. I had enough to deal with myself.

I told Samih about my nightmare. He said that there was no way to relate dreams to reality and that, in general, dreams were future oriented rather than a storehouse of the past. I asked him to explain further, so he said, "I don't know exactly, but I once heard on the radio about Russian research that found that, astonishingly, more than 70 percent of our dreams forecast future events in our lives."

By now, I didn't feel awkward asking him how he saw dreams. He told me that he found it hard to explain the things he saw, that he sensed things more than he could describe them in terms of specific structures and figures, and that the colors that people talked about had no place in his dreams. He did not give the matter much importance, and the moment he woke, his dreams disappeared. He advised me to train myself to forget the things that were disturbing me because time would erase them.

SIX DAYS PASSED. I spent that time trying to run away from Moosa's face, which was following me like a question mark. Tomorrow we would meet as we had agreed, but this time I would have to have made a decision.

What was I going to do if I was still undecided? I was
both drawing him close to me and pushing him away. I
feared losing him and was running from him. The last
time I had seen him, he had made me face myself, and
tomorrow it would be up to me to say my final word. I
searched for a clear reason for my confusion. Why was
I so headstrong regarding my heart? What was making
me afraid of giving things a try? I had originally justified
my indecision by saying that my rejection or acceptance
of Moosa would be determined by the rejection or acceptance of my refugee status. It had been a test for my feelings; I hadn't wanted to say yes just because I had been
rejected. I had told Moosa, "Let me think; give me time
to make a decision. What you don't know is that I'm stubborn when the situation calls for me to say yes. Unfortunately, I did not say it when I was in Baghdad." He had
told me that what happens in politics does not apply to
the heart and suggested that perhaps I was running away
from him or didn't want to hurt his feelings. What would
I tell him tomorrow?

I was confused and split into two women: one attached to the past's bitterness and the other taking me
into an unknown tomorrow. The first one was bound
by faded threads to her grandmother; the second carried a sharp knife and was cutting those threads. But
my grandmother would come to me in the crevices of
night, her face pale and clear, her body like the trunk of
a palm tree; she would begin by whispering and then
would scream with her natural instinct that was never
mistaken, "You are lying! You are leaving for a faraway
place, far from al-Najaf!" She would then die down like a
flickering candle, patting me on the shoulder and saying

in a soft voice, "Youssef no longer has a place in your heart. Have mercy on yourself and have mercy on your memory of me."

The other woman cried out, "I'm tired of the smells of a bed where one body has succeeded another and too many desires have been shared." Then she took me to a future wrapped in thick fog, in which I desperately searched for the beats of my paralyzed heart. The question of what would be next in my life was hurting me. It became even more painful: what had become of me? A woman in her thirties trying to be in control of her life, fighting for a place in this world, but feeling a fear that inhibited her steps; every time she got close to hope, despair plagued her, and every time she decided something, the decision would be extinguished by hesitation.

"Why do I look only at the dark aspects of life?" I asked myself. "Things are not so bad. I shouldn't close the doors of hope, only to peer out, like a spectator, through windows that let in smoke that blinds me."

During that long, cold night, I held fast to my feelings. I stripped them of hazy illusions and discovered that Moosa's grip on my affections had become lighter. My feelings for him were like a slow-moving stream when I was longing for a strong, overflowing river. A voice echoed from far away, "Was Youssef an overflowing river?" But I didn't halt to remember those feelings that had been broken just by crossing the homeland's border. I was still chasing Moosa, trying to find a way to reshape my feelings toward him. My God, what was so mysterious about this man? I was unable to steer my own ship, so why shouldn't I let another captain steer it? What was it that I really wanted?

Outside the room, the wailing wind played with the trees, making fearful sounds. The impetuous rain first pounded on the door with violence, then knocked quietly. My toes stiffened, and the cold spread to my bones. The smells of the bed, which I had gotten used to, pierced my senses once again. The other woman was forcing her way into my mind, firing my memory so that the past was rising like hair on my skin. The past was attacking like a thief, striking me fiercely.

My heart burned as little things glimmered in my memory: my home's furniture, my grandmother's stories, and my mother's spirit, which would roam through the house despite her eternal absence. Oh, God, what was this spiral in which I was trapped? I was constantly returning to the point from which I had begun. The night's hours were shapeless, agonizing, lonely, anxiously bringing forth both dark and luminous images. I was like a blind person fumbling through eternal darkness. I could see a playing child nibbling barefoot on red mulberries. I reached my hand toward her, but she slipped away, and her features faded behind thick black smoke that enveloped me as I ran from it. I plunged once more into memories that mercilessly stripped off my skin. The Factory of Hope crossed my mind. I remembered Shafiqa scourging us with her commanding voice. I longed for the arguments between Mother Khadija and Salwa. Aziza appeared before me with her lofty looks and refined temperament. I wondered if she still dreamed of marrying a man in order to escape poverty, siege, and the land of wars, as she had called it.

The clock's ticktock knocked at my head. I washed away all the pictures and cleared a path for the other woman, who had returned from the depths of my soul, crying, "Moosa, open a clear way for me with your stick and wipe away your secret mystery. You, creature whose riddles I'm unable to decipher, why do I wander with you in a vicious circle? What do you hide behind your deep eyes? Show me how to determine my way and pass into yours without being wounded. I wish you had revealed to me the secrets of your life so that I could know what kind of man I might be journeying with, but you say little when it comes to specifics, as though you are fleeing from something you want to forget and clinging to whatever will grant you forgetfulness."

The wind was still swirling outside, but the rain had stopped. I didn't think I would sleep before dawn, but then I woke up and remembered that I had dreamed of Nadia. She had been walking a spiral, her arms folded over her notebook, which she had hugged to her chest. I had been following her without her knowing, and when she noticed my footsteps, she became frightened and began to run until she disappeared behind a door surrounded by barbed wire. As I caught up to her and stepped to the entrance, a thick fog had rushed upon me and then cleared, revealing endless emptiness.

It was seven in the morning. I looked at Nadia's notebook on top of the books and began to reflect on the dream. She had been angry. She was still angry with me. I had fallen into confusion; she surely was attacking me, as if I had committed a great offense against her. Oh, God! What might it be?

WE WERE SITTING on a green wooden bench near hundred-year-old stone pillars. I was staring at the columns that mocked our lives, which were nothing in the scale of time.

Moosa put a leather satchel on his lap. I could hear him saying, "I missed you. I didn't sleep last night."

"Me either," I said, still looking at the stone pillars.

A light, chilly wind was playing with the cypress branches, and children were shouting and playing ball near us. Noisy families busy with their own concerns sat on other benches. It was Friday, and everyone was free of duties. People were walking slowly as they entered and exited the Roman amphitheater, eating sandwiches, drinking juice. The tea vendor was carrying his teapot, hawking his merchandise. I didn't need anyone to point out the Iraqi faces; they were easy to find in Amman, sharing feelings of homesickness. Plus, Iraqis use a singular dialect that doesn't resemble other Arabic dialects. I heard Moosa saying, "I feel as if I haven't seen you for ages."

I didn't know what to reply. It was the first time that he had talked about his longing for me. I kept quiet. I was looking for something lost inside me, wondering how love springs from our skins to become a hurricane that upsets the soul's balance and plays with the heart's rhythm. How far I was from that! Why wouldn't love flourish in exile? Why were its embers dying and failing to warm the limbs? Was love mistaking the time and place? Where was the warmth of things around us? Was I heeding my grandmother's warning to hold the stick from its middle? How could I explain my longing for Moosa every time I retreated to my room? Did I just need him? Did I need a man's company, separate from passion and desire? Moosa lifted me from my chaotic feelings as he broke the lengthy silence.

"Maybe I failed in the way I expressed my feelings; perhaps I should have asked, 'Are you engaged?'"

Although his question didn't surprise me, I defensively replied, "No!"

His eyes didn't believe me, so I went on, "I was engaged."

He lit a cigarette and began smoking slowly. "And now?"

"I'm free."

"Can I know more?"

"It's finished and doesn't worry me. Out of sight, out of mind, as they say."

"Are you sure about that?"

"Many things abide in us without our acceptance. For example, do we accept being here? More than three million have left Iraq since the Gulf War, scattered all over the world; hundreds of them died while they were dreaming of another country. Do you think they accepted it? Our feelings, too, rust with time's passing, and we need to make the effort to polish them."

"Feelings don't rust if they are made of solid materials. What we lose and what we miss leave their traces in the heart."

"What about you?"

"I was in a relationship. But years of flight, absence, life in the camps, poverty, and the passing of years, all that has made me another man. My views about life have changed. And since I have forever lost the woman I loved, I've reconsidered things in light of the circumstances in which I've found myself."

"We desire, but only fate draws and plans."

"But we shouldn't leave things to fate."

"Tell me about that woman, if you don't mind."

He threw away his cigarette butt. "She was extraordinary in every way. You remind me of her, but I'm not sure how—perhaps your calm or the way you talk or something else."

"Is that why you chose me?"

"No. When I saw you, I felt I needed you, and that need grew with time. When I saw you in difficulty, I made that offer."

I shrank into myself. He hadn't said he loved me. He'd said he needed me, but love is not a need; it is a feeling that overturns our thoughts and changes our lives' trajectories. Love is like a fever inhabiting our bones, a delicious fever, whereas need is dictated by circumstances, and in our case it was dictated by exile. I couldn't blame him for it when I had the same feeling. I needed him; I needed anybody who could tie down the loose thread of time.

Staring at one of the big stone blocks, I said, "I want to be honest with you. The mere word *offer* makes me feel base, exactly like a surplus item at a public sale."

He was shaken, and his eyes widened. "No . . . Perhaps I didn't express myself well. It is true that at first I only wanted to help you and save you from your predicament here. I had thought that the wedding contract would be a mere formality until you arrived in the new country and decided. But over time my feelings toward you have taken a different direction."

I waited until he lit another cigarette to say, "Don't you think that exile brings people closer to each other, causing them not to know their feelings, but that when things return to normal, they reconsider their hearts?"

"No," he said. "Sometimes exile increases dissension. I already told you that some of the Iraqis here in Amman came to spy and report on each other. Imagine. I have a friend; I fled with him after the failed uprising. We suffered together during the journey's hardships, drank putrid water, and ate the forest grass while fleeing. We entered refugee camps in Iran, got sick, suffered beyond what men can bear, and then suddenly his values collapsed, and he weakened. I found out that he was spying on others who were in our same situation. He would have died at the hands of the refugees if it hadn't been for the guards' intervention; they saved him while he was drowning in his blood."

As he was telling me about these atrocities, I scanned his face as though seeing him for the first time. I looked at his brown face and the scar over his left eyebrow. I plunged into his glowing eyes and his lips, which cigarettes had stained a dark color. I observed the words taking form and coming out hot and fresh from his mouth. I was drawn into him, looking for the other man in him.

"Forget about all this," I said to him. "Let's return to our original subject. I don't deny that I need you, too, and a huge emptiness fills my soul when I don't see you for a long time. But I can't deceive myself; I'm afraid my loneliness is making me grasp at straws."

This time I was the one who had expressed herself poorly. A thread of sadness spun in his eyes, and he fell silent, as if collecting his thoughts.

"I don't wish to be a straw. Believe me, I would rather be a lifeboat or a captain leading you to firm land. Give me a chance to prove my sincerity."

"Then open up to me. You lock so much away."

He extinguished his cigarette and said, smiling, "I don't know what you're looking for. I don't think I'm hiding anything. Here I am, in your hands, an open book ready for you to read slowly."

With coquetry, I said, "What about the woman you loved? Over time, won't true love dig deep into your heart and not leave any place for me?"

"No one can deny his past. We can't erase our memories, but this doesn't mean that once our first love is over, we can't fall in love again. When life denies us one thing, it gives us other choices; the past becomes merely a pleasant echo that settles in the soul."

He seemed convincing, and I felt he had crept closer to my feelings, although I was still looking for his hidden face. I looked at him carefully, hoping to find his secret, but it remained hidden. Then he cornered me with a question I had been afraid to ask myself. "What is the truth of your feelings toward me?"

Confused, I shifted a little bit on the bench. He was making me face my heart, which I had been dodging and deceiving. I bowed my head silently, then lifted it, but before I could say anything, a boy's cries arose as he fell among the rocks. His mother hurriedly stood up, saying, "God save you!"

She had spoken without knowing that she planted thorns in my heart. The father rushed over, horrified, and hugged the child. Then the mother grabbed her son, hugging him to her chest.

I said to Moosa, "Did you hear what the mother said?"

He looked at me inquiringly without responding, so I said, "'God save you.' It's an expression only Iraqis say.

Do you think we would hear it in Australia or in Canada or in the Netherlands or . . . ?"

Laughing, he interrupted me. "If you want, I'll say it to you ten times a day."

He repeated himself firmly. "You didn't answer my question. I'd like to know your true feelings; otherwise, we will not meet again."

He wasn't giving me the opportunity to hold the stick in its middle. I said, as I felt myself give in, "I don't want you to only narrowly enter my heart. I feel an inclination toward you, but I don't understand the nature of this inclination. I'm afraid."

"Are you afraid of me? Or am I outside the requirements of your heart?"

"We can no longer look at requirements and criteria as we used to do. I'm not afraid of you exactly, but I'm afraid of everything around me. I'm not adjusted to the time and place, and this is making it more difficult to adjust to my feelings. I am living a life that was imposed on me, and so it regulates my feelings. Why don't you give us some time to better know our feelings toward each other? Let's meet and talk. You know, you are sparring with words, and this diminishes our chances."

A ball rolled between our feet. Moosa grabbed it and gave it to the child who stood there, staring at us with shy eyes as though apologizing; then he looked at me and spoke.

"When it comes to feelings, chitchat is deadly. If I were to tell you everything, the conversation would end before it even began. Sometimes I feel I'm too old to do that, despite the burning feelings inside me. I've been through tumultuous times, and I've put up with wounds during the war and the difficult work in the refugee camps. The wars I experienced also made me forget love's language, which we used to master. I experienced ferocious battles in which I would have rather died than kill another soldier like me, who had a father, a mother, and dreams awaiting him. I walked all the way back from Kuwait in humiliation and shame. I experienced the uprising and then the flight to Iran through al-Ahwaz. There we lived as though we were prisoners of war."

I expressed my surprise and asked him how that was possible.

He explained, "In Iran, political asylum for Iraqis is not recognized and is therefore illegal. Iraqis have no right to travel or to marry an Iranian woman or to work, even though the Iranian Constitution guarantees a foreign resident of ten years the right to work. Even the Iraqi children who grow up there cannot pursue their studies. They call us 'uninvited guests who have outstayed their welcome,' and they see us as a burden on Iran; there is no way for us to stay. We were refugees, but in barbed-wire prisons. I and a few others who were closer to the border were employed illegally, doing humiliating jobs for very little money. My earnings of three years were given to one of the smugglers so I could come here, hoping to join my brother, who migrated to Australia as soon as I arrived."

"Did you participate in the uprising?"

"Yes. I had returned from Kuwait disappointed and humiliated, and my other brother had been killed on the uprising's third day, although he'd been unarmed. He was a student and was put to death along with twenty other students in the university square. Because I was wanted by the authorities, I assumed his name when I fled. I kept my brother's name in order to preserve his memory, never retaking my real name. I live now with my brother's life, the life that could have continued if they hadn't killed him. From a young age, I had always wanted to be him because he had been an extraordinary person. Sometimes I feel guilty for having wished that—I wonder if God preserved my life so that I could live out my brother's life. But now my soul has become peaceful, and I feel that every time I bury my own name, I reenact that faithfulness to his memory. I loved him very much."

It didn't occur to me to ask him what his previous name was. It wasn't important; I knew him by the name "Moosa," and that was it. We carry names for identification, and when the name becomes a death threat, we have to write it off.

I looked at Moosa; he was pale and looked profoundly sad. He was rubbing his palms anxiously as his gaze became harsh; I felt as if I had scraped the scab from his wounds. He started to smoke nervously. I was thinking of excusing myself when he stood up, saying, "Let's sit in a quiet place."

We walked silently. I felt his sadness creeping into my chest and pressing it. Every time I met him, the conversation would stir up sadness and sorrow, and I wasn't sure why. I thought about retreating to my room to punish myself. I heard him say, "Are you with me?"

While I was withdrawn from him, he had wanted to say something. We reached the café, and he signaled the waiter, who came quickly.

"What do you want to drink?"

"Tea."

"Two teas, please."

He continued smoking, scanning every corner as if looking for something. Then, as if postponing the conversation about his suffering, he said, "Listen. I don't want to drown myself or you with the weight of the past. What do you think?"

He opened the leather satchel and took out a bundle of papers. "Read these at home, and let's enjoy our meeting now. I am excusing you from answering my question. We are friends now, just friends, if it's okay with you. We'll meet here tomorrow morning and speak more freely. Is ten o'clock good for you?"

He had eliminated the pressure on me, and I smiled at him; his face looked calm. The harshness in his gaze was disappearing, and he had stopped twisting his palms. At this very moment, I wished I could be in love with him and could feverishly cry on his shoulder. I felt my feelings flaring up again, but I controlled my heart's unruliness. I feared myself and my mood changes—I was pushing him away whenever he approached and then trying to draw him closer whenever he stopped discussing our relationship. As we parted, my palm was between his; I could feel something inside me moving and wanting to catch him, but we separated, going our own separate ways.

I wanted to cry on the street; I fought to overcome this feeling as I looked at the shops and kiosks. These sidewalk stands were managed by Iraqi women who were spending the end of their lives in strange streets. Each time I encountered one of these women, a desire rose up in me to sit down and talk to her as if she were my mother or my grandmother; these women were part of the beautiful past that rekindled those sweet stories that spilled from the lips of our grandmothers.

I stopped near a very old sad woman selling incense sticks, napkins, cigarettes, and Indian hair dye. She was arranging her merchandise on a black rug. I bought some incense that I didn't need and looked carefully at her features. Her face reminded me of my mother's, which I had almost forgotten.

Trying to stretch out the conversation between us, I said to the woman, "This stuff is not worth going into exile for."

Without looking at me, she replied, "What should I do? I'm entertaining myself while I wait for the end of my days."

"You would do better to have fun there, in the Iraqi public markets."

She looked at me harshly as she replied, "What do you want? Are you one of them?"

Taken aback, I said, "God forbid. Do I look like them?"

She replied in a softer tone, "I don't know. I'm unable to tell. All of us have worries. We came to Amman to display our sorrows, but no one buys sorrows."

"I'm like you, Grandma."

"No, you are not like me. You are young; life is before you; you can make up for what you missed. But for the likes of me, God alone knows what we suffer. Are you married? Do you have children?"

"No, I'm uprooted."

"What prompted you to talk with me? Everyone who buys goes on his way."

I looked at the tattoos between her brows and on her cheeks and said, "You look like my mother."

She answered carelessly, "Where is your mother?"

"She died a long time ago; she didn't go through the wars that we went through."

"That's better; at least in her old age she preserved her dignity. As for us, you can see we have become a spectacle, selling our sorrow in the streets. I'm a mother of four. Two of them died in the war with Iran; the third was lost in the war with Kuwait, and the fourth is here with me. He works with a shoemaker in Saqf al-Sayl."

All of a sudden, though, she shook herself, gathered her goods, and disappeared up an alley, saying, "The police, the police."

There was nothing left in her place except her shoes. She hadn't had time to put them on.

WHEN I GOT HOME, I had a snack, eager to look at Moosa's papers. After I finished eating, I shut the curtain, propped the pillow up against the headboard, and leaned back comfortably. I reached for the papers and began.

Dear Huda,

I am sharing my wounds with you, although for many years I have tried to bury them in the hope of sparing myself their cruel assault. I didn't want to recount them as others do, always carrying their sadness and spreading it until it fades from repetition. I'm the kind of person who never gives up in the face of calamities. I have written down some of the events I have gone through, and it's the subject of a book that will have the title *Diary of a Soldier Returning from the Defeat.* Here, I have chosen for you part of that story, which is as painful as many other parts. Please, read slowly. It describes what we went through. The next generations have the right to know the catastrophe's impact before someone denies them this right to the truth.

Best wishes.

After this letter, which Moosa had clearly written yesterday, I began reading the pages he had given me.

Back from death, balls of fire, shrapnel, burning vehicles, and cluster bombs, I was back from moving death, where the lines of retreating vehicles had become an excellent target for airplanes. The vehicles burned along with the bodies. The storm of explosions had thrown soldiers onto the roads, dead and mangled or wounded and helpless. They remained grim faced, looking toward the horizon and waiting for their deaths. Yet these men were actually luckier than those who were being crushed at night by the tanks and heavy-armored cars. The latter were frozen pieces of tissue and bone. I'm back from this horrible chaos, from all this doom. It was only by accident that I escaped the killing.

We had set forth in a vehicle that was taking us from al-Zubayr in Basra to release and reenlist us in Baghdad. This happened at the same time as the withdrawal from Kuwait. The long convoy had left the large al-Zubayr Square, and the soldiers walked dazedly in the mud of defeat. Indeed, there was a lot of mud, for it hadn't stopped raining for three days. The soldiers plunged into the mud, away from the main road, which was always targeted by airplanes. The continuous chain of hundreds of soldiers hurried with sinking steps to Basra, while fire devoured some of the vehicles and bodies fell dead from them. It was absurdly surreal when a dog rushed to a body and began to devour it just before a passerby hurried to shoot him dead next to the body!

We quickly crossed to al-Zubayr Bridge, which had been blown up in the first days by the air raids. A sandy dam along the bridge was the only way to cross Shatt al-Basra, which collects the waters of central and southern Iraq and discharges them into the sea. The mud stretched to that sandy barricade, and burning vehicles and armored cars blocked the way. A soldier's body was hanging from a vehicle similar to ours, left on the side of the road; the tank was wet with rain, and red drops were falling from it, forming rosy lines on the mud. The dead man was facing the ground, so I could make out only a hanging trunk and swollen limbs.

Our driver skillfully crossed the road around the steel carcasses, stopping at the end of the line of vehicles crossing the sandy dam. One of our vehicles sank into the mud in the middle of the road, making it impossible for the rest of us to reach the other bank. We became an ideal target for an air strike.

I jumped from the vehicle; my feet plunged into the mud as I passed under a low, black cloud that was rising from a burning oil well. The roar of an approaching plane meant another fire and explosion that would obliterate many of the bodies packed here. A tractor—I don't know where it suddenly came from or how its driver kept his calm—hooked a chain to our sunken vehicle and pulled it back to the other bank. I and the other soldiers who had abandoned our vehicle jumped back into it.

The line of refugees grew longer as we approached Basra. As we stopped for a wounded person who was piteously asking for a ride, many other tired soldiers hurried to the vehicle. When we reached Sa'd's Square, Basra's landmark for Iraqi soldiers, the extent of the chaos became clear to us: in the middle of town there were tanks everywhere, heavy artillery was on the sidewalks, and soldiers were chewing bread on the street. I shifted my gaze to the features of the city itself. Young girls were looking down from an apartment balcony, witnessing what was going on in the street. The roof of the Basra television and media headquarters had been blown up by a huge missile, and the damage to the building seemed extensive. Just ahead of us, a clamoring tank suddenly stopped and turned to the right, discharging a heavy shower of bullets at a huge portrait of the president. I was floored by this act. "Something is going to happen here," I said to myself.

We arrived at al-Ishar. It was noisy, not because of its usual daily activity as the lively center of Basra, but because of the crowd of soldiers moving from sidewalk to sidewalk, square to square, and bridge to bridge. The corniche was choked with soldiers who were trying to cross Shatt el-Arab on their way to Tannuma. We left, heading to the small bridge that leads to the shrine of Imam Ali. The chaos rose to a fury as soldiers on the sidewalks and between cars crowded into parallel lines, trying to cross a temporary bridge set up over Shatt el-Arab. The hundreds of vehicles were barely moving. What a massacre there would be if an air strike were made against us right then! No sooner did I think this than the thunder of an approaching plane incited a panic.

Like terrified worms on the ground, we jumped from the vehicles to the streets nearby or under the small bridge; some soldiers threw themselves on the riverbank. Piled with stones from Basra's Reconstruction Campaign, the bank was paradoxically witnessing the Destruction Campaign against the Iraqi people. Our fear drove us aimlessly into a bottleneck. A young woman on one of the balconies, unfolding her laundry, gazed at our featureless faces.

From three until seven that night, we waited for the huge line of vehicles to move. I was struck by the scene. Crowds of soldiers were crossing the bridge, walking to Shatt el-Arab's other bank. I asked the pedestrians, "Where to?"

"To my house" . . . "To Baghdad" . . . "To al-Hilla" . . . "To Kirkuk" . . . "To Ramadi" . . . "To Karbala" . . . The sunset trailed dark threads, adding more gloom to the desolation of the cold and the thick mud.

I leaned on one of the walls overlooking the strange street scenes. Old men emerged, dazed, and women began to distribute water to the soldiers. Despite their poverty, some families didn't hesitate to hand out hot tea and pieces of bread. Then a man in his thirties came out with his two daughters. They stared at me, but I could hardly smile. After a few moments, one of the girls began to cry. (Cry, you little girl. Let anything come out of you; let something come out to change this horror, so that the sound of life postpones the rhythm of death and defeat.)

We eventually crossed to the other bank. On the road, through orchards of date palms, the driver called out the number of our unit so that soldiers could make their way to us and continue their journey. Many groups showed up—some we knew, and others we didn't—and for a moment they seemed like horrifying creatures emerging from their tombs. They were wrapped in blankets, and the darkness added to their strange, ghostly aspect. We arrived at Tannuma, and its only street was crowded with vehicles and soldiers. I thought about spending the night at my aunt's place there, but I didn't stop.

We took the road to Katiban through groves of palm trees. Along the way, I saw soldiers walking barefoot. I didn't know how they would be able to continue or when they would give up. This was the same road that had taken up a great deal of my life during the eight-year war with Iran: the battles of East Basra between 1982 and 1984, Majnun, al-Nashwa, Buhayrat al-Asmaak, al-Fao with its farms, and the Shalamja . . . and . . . and . . . And here again were the hands of death, taking me and thirty other soldiers in a vehicle through the darkness in silence.

At the crossroad between al-Nashwa and Majnun, the procession stopped. The vehicles were motionless in a long line on the road. No one knew the reason for the halt, but I sensed the smell of death close to us. I yelled to those who were with me, "Get down quickly!" From a gap in the clouds obstructing a bright moon, two planes appeared. I hurried to reach a small canal and threw myself into the mud. The explosions resounded; shrapnel flew above my head, and four men up the canal were motionless after a slight rattle. Fire devoured the unmoving line, but our vehicle seemed safe. The planes came back. It was dreadful. I wanted to sleep—yes, to close my eyes and sleep. Fatigue and weakness overcame my whole body, and I no longer feared anything. Let it be enough, come what may.

With ten other soldiers, between one attack and another, I headed to an abandoned house in the middle of an orchard of palm trees. The driver of the vehicle, Talib Halil, the calmest of us in the midst of horror, had returned to the burning line and brought back his personal weapon, my bag, and some blankets. He handed me a blanket and said, "Let's go to sleep; tomorrow is another day." How could I sleep with this flying horror that never ceased? I dropped to the cold earth in exhaustion. I spread half of the blanket on the ground and covered my body with the other half.

Morning came with the effects of fire all around us. Bodies drilled with shrapnel were thrown on the side of the road; the scorched corpses reeked in a day devoid of life. Some peasants walked on the road, looking around to see what was happening. We continued walking between burned vehicles, looking at propaganda portraits and official murals on the facade of the military road units. They had been sprayed by bullets from close range.

Burned or destroyed vehicles lay here and there. Slumberous bodies drenched in blood dangled from their sides. Other bodies had been abandoned on the streets. The earth itself seemed to have recoiled, ready to jump, to join us, another body about to be destroyed.

"Quickly, quickly, take us, Ibn Halil, while the fog is covering everything—we hope it will be our umbrella protecting us from the hell swarm of aluminum birds and their wild, rapacious claws. Oh! Morning of our drenched bodies! Shaking, terrified, and burning, poisoned, starved, yet young. And you, Sun, take your time, and please delay your threads of light."

This is how I was praying, like a Bedouin playing his rebec, swaying back and forth. But what kind of music could there ever be amid burned bodies?

The rubble of machinery and the bodies scattered around blocked our way. One of the tanks proceeded to open the road, pushing aside the bodies and piles of metal, and we quickly crossed through. But the same scene repeated itself at the Majnun al-Hadidi Dam, which had recently been attacked before we reached it. The rubble was still warm. The thick smoke mixed with the fog and embraced the papyrus plants. The plants offered us a convenient refuge between their long stems, which rustled and leaned when the air was shaken by yet another fierce attack.

The shrapnel flew over my head, and I could hear someone calling for help not far away. I wanted to continue my way through the papyrus, following the streams, along the muddy earth and away from the dangers of the road, which had become a deadly trap. There the planes were finding an easy hunt for more bodies. But once again Talib Halil, our driver, made it safely from the fire and began to honk, calling us to jump in again.

I abandoned my original idea and jumped quickly into the vehicle, accompanied by wounded soldiers from another unit who were able to jump in as well. The same scene was repeating itself all along the road. Many fragments of bodies were scattered in the middle of the road, but I'll never forget the sight of one young soldier seated on the edge of the road with blood covering his shoulders and his back. He was looking toward the horizon and the stretch of grass and mud, moving his head in a familiar regretful way. He turned his back to us as the last light in his eyes mixed with the shreds of the dissipating fog. As we passed him, I looked through the window and followed the slow movement of his trunk back and forth. Oh, God, just a few minutes ago I had been moving like that. Was it the rhythm of the body's death? His hand was still pointing to the horizon, and his back was turned to the killing.

The sun overcame the fog, and morning came just when we had given up completely; we set out, but to where? We were desperate; two airplanes roamed once more over our heads, wings shining under the sun. I warned the driver that we needed to stop and get out of the vehicle. We scattered in small groups between the folds of the earth, and its green grass embraced our bodies and welcomed our fear with its freshness.

I stood on a sandy hill as the others moved away from me and hurried into the depths. I could see four missiles dropping on our small groups. At that moment, I found myself reproaching my mother's soul, which had appeared to me in my dreams two days earlier. She had told me that I would get back home safely. I asked her, "Mama, how could you have foretold my safety when death is here, falling on me, buzzing, with its wings open wide?" I saw the missile hit four vehicles in the road, where we had split in two directions. Shrapnel flew, and our vehicle was trapped between two fires as we stared at it as if it called to us: "Come on, let's go. The journey is long."

Sudden cries rose up, coming from what remained of the groups of soldiers. The scene was one of hysteria—soldiers embracing each other, then separating and covering their faces with their palms. Vehicles began to stop, and soldiers walked back and forth: jumping, embracing, crying out. Plucking up my courage, I reassembled my shattered self and tried to walk but felt unable to move, as if my back were still broken. I realized how perfect that expression was for describing a fate-stricken person. Indeed, my back was broken, and my country's back was broken too. When I reached those groups, I learned that a cease-fire would go into effect at 8:00 a.m.—in just two minutes. How could they have been killing us only five minutes earlier? Five minutes had separated many young men from life. I threw myself on the side of a dried stream and looked for my cigarettes. I took one and caressed it with my fingers, inhaling its smoke deeply; I could hardly hold it with my shaking fingers.

I pulled myself together and catapulted my body forward. Others made it ahead of me to the vehicle crossing the road. Crying together, we left the fire behind, along with the remnants of our brothers. We wailed in mourning; we entered the gates of the small southern towns, whose people came out at our sudden appearance, inquiring about what had happened, about a son, a brother, a husband, and about us.

Many women scattered sand on top of their heads, and others beat their chests with their hands in a historical reenactment of the killings that had always taken place there. The towns we entered seemed very strange and bitter. This time, defeat had been declared. As we made our way to one town's center, a young boy welcomed us with the sign of victory, but he purposely put it upside down.

"Yes, little boy, you are right. The mud of our defeat is what we brought to you. You have to look for a way that starts from here, from the chaos of this bloody return."[12]

When I emerged from these bloody pages, I was weeping in horror. Although I was familiar with most of what had happened, I still sank into a deep sorrow. I lay there shivering until I fell into a deep sleep, as if my head, crowded with scenes of horror, had shaken off everything and become empty. When I woke up and looked in the mirror, I was pale, as though sick. It was four o'clock.

WHEN FIANCA, the maid, opened the door to me, I heard Samiha's voice welcoming me from the living room. She was lying on the couch, suffering from back pain. She told me about some faded memories that I wasn't interested in hearing about. I tried to listen to her, but Moosa kept intruding.

Samiha told me that she needed to stay home. *(Moosa reiterates, "I jumped from the vehicle; my feet plunged into the*

---

12. The material quoted is from a diary of an Iraqi soldier, poet Ali Abd el-Emir, dated March 2, 1991.

mud.") Samiha sat with a pillow behind her back, moaning. *(Moosa says that the soldiers along the streets walked barefoot.)* She said, "If I have to go see the doctor, I'd like you to come with me." *(Moosa's voice slips in: a morning of fire and bodies drilled with shrapnel.)* Fianca told me that Samih was waiting for me. *(Moosa reminds me of our appointment the next day)*. Samiha pointed to a pile of newspapers on the table. *(Moosa asks me about the nature of my feelings toward him)*.

In the room decorated in Arabian style, Samih sat near his lute, smiling as usual. Fianca set down two cups of coffee and two glasses of water.

"Today," he said, "no need to read. I think it's a day for chat."

This wasn't part of our contract, but I acquiesced and found it convenient. Samih asked me about what had happened at the Refugee Office and to which country I would be sent.

I answered, "Perhaps I will go to Australia, the other side of the world."

He said, "There is a shining place waiting for you."

I didn't know why he said that, so I asked, "Do you think things will be okay?"

"You'll have to adjust. I've heard that the standard of living there is one of the highest; it's the country of pineapple, natural resources, and virgin land. People there live in the present, whereas we hold on to our sorrows."

I said to him, "We—I mean 'I'—need a decent present in order to continue. The absence of an enticing present leaves us no choice but to discuss our memories time and again."

Samih objected. "There are many incentives for the present, but we don't acknowledge them. They are with us, within and around us, but our insight—I mean your insight—is obstructed. But isn't that what you've been wishing for? At least you don't have to worry about your relocation."

"Worry never ends. It might recede, but it never ends, not just for me, but for all Iraqis—those who live under the regime's hammer and those who have left the country looking for another life."

"God will help you."

"It looks as if this is our destiny—a diaspora growing bigger over the years."

"No, things are different from what you think. If every dissident left the country, that would give the ruler, who had brought calamities upon the country, a new, longer life."

"What you say is true, but many were forced to do exactly that. The world knows only what it sees on television screens or in newspapers. The details of our lives and misfortune are known only to us. As for me, you know my problem; although I have nothing to do with politics and don't even understand its games, I am entrapped in its snare. I'm a woman who longs for a peaceful life: a house, a husband and children, reading and intimate relationships. Unfortunately, I have found myself outside these dreams. I don't know how to handle what has happened to me, but my people's cause is a tragedy, and I'm merely a small part of it."

I wanted to tell Samih that a man had entered my life at the wrong time and that my feelings toward him were mixed. At that very instant, I wanted to fly to that man, but I was afraid that when I arrived, my wings would fall apart. I decided not to tell Samih about him.

I looked at Samih. He was silent. I didn't know if he was with me or in another place. When he spoke, his voice was sad. "If you emigrate, I'll find it difficult to adjust to another person."

"There's nothing extraordinary about me. I just do my work. Wasn't there a woman before me doing the same job?"

He said in a low voice, "You're different."

He lapsed into silence before he said, "You arouse my feelings." Then he emended, "Sorry. I hope you don't get me wrong—I'm in love with your voice." Then he said, "Don't misinterpret; I just wanted to say that with you I see things better."

Before he could return to his lute, I said, "There are specialized centers where they teach blind people how to read with the computer. Why don't you sign up?"

He said, "I don't feel close to a computer; it doesn't have a soul, and I can't have a dialogue with it. I believe in intimate and warm relationships." Then he grabbed his lute and began to strum on it. A delicate echo of sadness wafted from it. The chords called for relaxation and harmony with nature, then became more intricate, forming a melody that rose and carried me high. I could see myself galloping on a green meadow, like a horse freed from her reins. I could see colorful images I'd never seen before. The lute suddenly fell silent and left me stranded.

ON THE WAY TO HASHEMITE SQUARE, I met the same woman who had previously been sitting on the sidewalk. Next to her was another woman selling loofahs, black bath stones, tweezers, and needles. I wasn't paying attention to her face as I greeted the two women and sat. But before I could extend my hand to the incense sticks, the second woman shrieked, "Huda?"

The world is like a village; fate leads its dwellers to meet one another. But it is also as large as an endless universe, where each human is just a dot lost in the emptiness. In Amman, you may run into a neighbor or a friend or any other person you have met during the journey of your life, but in your own country you may not meet that person for years. Everybody here, especially in the downtown area and Hashemite Square, became a familiar face as long as we all carried the same tragedy. A faded cloak and intertwined wrinkles like an old tree—that was Mother Khadija.

I shrieked too. "Who? Mother Khadija? I can't believe it!"

She hugged me like a daughter. I could feel her warm breaths on my chest.

"Even you, Mother Khadija! What brought you here?"

With the corner of her cloak, she was wiping her tears. "What could I do? I found myself destitute after the fire at the Factory of Hope; no one paid attention to me. All my friends had gone to a safe haven. Life is better here, except for the problems of residence."

"And where do you live?"

"At Talát al-Misdaar with Umm Hashim." She pointed to her neighbor.

Umm Hashim replied, "We share the rent, we eat together, and . . ." She wanted to say more but then became busy with a customer.

Mother Khadija was holding my fingers and squeezing them with affection. Then she asked, "And you, what are you doing here?"

"I'm on the waiting list."

She looked at me as though she didn't understand what I meant. I added, "I'm a refugee; I'm going to a Western country."

"Which country?"

"I don't know yet. Australia or Holland or maybe America or Canada."

"Did you say America?"

"Yes, perhaps America or another country."

She stroked her chest as she asked a second time, "America, who hit us with missiles?"

"If they accept me."

"Things are so strange in this life—people seeking refuge with their killers."

I said to her, "Mother Khadija, the killers have become numerous now, and the worst of them is he who emerges from your own homeland."

She didn't look convinced and said, "Despite this, we should not seek refuge from the bad only to fall prey to worse."

"As Amin Maalouf puts it, the worst ruler is he who makes you hit yourself with the stick."

"Who is Amin Maalouf?"

"Huh? He's one of my relatives."

Umm Hashim was listening but did not interrupt. I continued, "Who said that America is worse than our president? America wasn't alone when she hit us; more than twenty countries had allied with her, including many Arab countries. It is our president who invaded an Arab country, looted it, and chased away its people. Anyway, Mother Khadija, don't worry about that because I'm actually going to Australia."

"I haven't heard of Australia. How far is it from here?"

"It is at the end of the world."

She opened her eyes wide. "The end of the world. That must be close to the day of resurrection."

Umm Hashim joined in the laughter. Mother Khadija, holding me as if she were afraid of losing me, began to lament, "Oh, my daughter, our people are scattered like the beads of a broken necklace! No one can reunite us! It is God's will; perhaps it's a punishment because we have lost the purity of our soul."

Umm Hashim objected, "On the contrary, we are the noblest people on earth—kind, tolerant, and generous."

Mother Khadija looked around her angrily, "Aren't we the descendants of al-Hajjaj?"[13]

Umm Hashim disagreed, "Al-Hajjaj is not from Iraq! You old folks!"

Before the debate could get too heated, I excused myself. It was time to meet Moosa.

Mother Khadija squeezed my palm and said, "We should keep in touch. You can always find me here, and if we have to move, I'll be near Restaurant al-Quds."

As I stood up, I said, "We'll see each other a lot, I promise."

She replied, "I hope that's not mere talk."

HE HAD ARRIVED in the café before me; from far away I could see him reading some papers. As I drew closer, he

13. Al-Hajjaj ibn Yusuf: an important provincial governor in Iraq during the Umayyad Empire whose methods of rule were very harsh and unpopular.

pushed his papers aside, saying, "This time my intuition betrayed me; I thought you wouldn't come."

I put my bag on the table's right side, asking, "What made you think that?"

"Frankly, yesterday you didn't look enthusiastic."

"Here I am."

"Your behavior confuses me."

Pulling the pages of his story from my bag, I said, "I was saddened by what you wrote. After all that has happened to you, I wonder how you've managed to preserve your soul."

I suddenly jumped with alarm when he grabbed my fingers. I turned my head but didn't withdraw my hands. I let them absorb the warmth of his feelings; I was in need of a man's caress. Pearls of sweat shone on his forehead. I wondered where this abundant flow of love that immersed my senses came from. The waiter interrupted this unplanned moment in a time of exile.

We ordered juice, and he read to me what he had written during his days in exile. Then we went to a fast-food place. He didn't ask me about my feelings toward him. Then he said, "Time is short. Should I add your name to my file? If you have reached a decision, give me a call after tomorrow, but if I don't hear from you, I'll consider the matter over with."

I was about to bypass the two-day waiting period and accept immediately, but for some reason I just kept silent.

MY SHIP WAS SAFE from being tossed over. A strength I had lacked for a long time flowed back into my body. I had received the refugee certificate.

I began scanning the lines. I couldn't believe it. "The Office for Refugee Affairs of the United Nations in the Jordanian Kingdom attests that Mrs. Huda Abdel Baqi, Iraqi citizen, is granted the status of Refugee . . ."

I wanted to shout in the streets, "Farewell to the nightmare of homelessness!" I wanted to tell the whole universe about it, to go back home and wait for Samih, or to fly to the Roman Theater and enter the Hashemite Square to announce it to the Iraqis there, but instead I walked to see Mother Khadija. I spotted Umm Hashim sitting in front of her merchandise in her usual place. As I bought incense from her, she told me that Mother Khadija was sick. I asked for directions to her place.

From Saqf al-Sayl, I walked to Mosque al-Husain in the northern part of the city, up to Talát al-Misdaar, then turned left as Umm Hashim had indicated. An iron door opened up to a relatively long corridor that eventually led to a circular basin that collected water, which was so scarce in that region. Mother Khadija was living in one of the three rooms that overlooked the sandy yard. I looked for her door. When a woman came out, I asked for Mother Khadija.

She pointed, saying, "The last room."

Mother Khadija couldn't believe it when she saw me. "What brought you here? By God, you are great."

She had wrapped herself in a blanket and sat close to the fireplace. She looked very pale.

"It's the cold," she said. "My bones can't tolerate it."

The room she shared with Umm Hashim was wide, with a corridor leading to the kitchen. Near the fire was a carafe with chamomile tea. She asked me to pour her a little bit to moisten her throat. She was dehydrated and had a slight fever. Then she pushed aside the blankets and cursed the time that had brought her to this condition. I didn't know what to say as she assured me that as soon as she felt better, she would return to Baghdad. She was afraid to die on foreign soil.

She sighed and said, "Oh, beloved Baghdad—abundant water, sunny weather, and people united as if they were one tribe. But they destroyed it. God's curse upon them! The idea of dying here frightens me. What do you think—should I die here?"

Patting her shoulders, I said, "God give you long life!"

She shivered. "No. I just want to reach Baghdad; then I don't care."

I told her about Nadia's death. She remembered her and said, "She was very kind and educated like you. She avoided the bickering that went on in the factory and preserved her purity."

She didn't ask about the circumstances of Nadia's death but continued to grieve and reminisce about the Factory of Hope, the workers, and Shafiqa, whose power had been broken after the factory was burned and Mr. Fatih had run away.

"Did Mr. Fatih really flee with millions of dollars?" I asked Mother Khadija. She poured some chamomile tea, took some sips, and went on, "God alone knows; there are no definite answers. I heard that he had entered the market. His rival was one of the president's cousins, so they asked him to back down from the deal, but he was too stubborn. He lost the deal and set the factory on fire. Rumors circulated that he took millions with him. But others said that he was arrested and perhaps put to death in prison."

Just one month before these events, I had left the factory and Nadia had moved to Basra.

"All this doesn't mean much to poor women. The world ignores us, while they are disgustingly rich. God curse them all!"

Mother Khadija's energy flowed as she discovered an unexpected desire to talk about those miserable days when our pay had barely supported our needs.

She sighed again and said, "Oh, my God, poor girls fighting for their bread. In our day, that wasn't the case. Every girl used to dream about marriage and motherhood. Fie on the bad times when women abandon their femininity for practices that degrade their dignity!" She looked at me and asked, "Have you heard anything about the other girls? What became of them?"

All this time, I'd wondered about the tense relationship between her and Salwa but couldn't find a way to broach the subject. Then I found myself asking the question from another angle. "I think they married; even the widowed and divorced among them would have looked for husbands."

She laughed mockingly. "Where from? The wars have eaten half of the men and left the other half handicapped or insane."

"They marry old men, although every one of them deserves to fulfill her dreams. Take, for example, Salwa."

Mother Khadija picked up the ball. "Salwa? Oh, hers is another story. I swear by God, I liked her."

"It didn't seem as if you liked each other."

"It wasn't my fault. She was ungrateful."

I tried to provoke her. "I think you were tough on her."

She looked embarrassed and said, "If it hadn't been for me, she would have died of shame."

I gave her a little shove and said, "No, no, Mother Khadija, what you're saying here isn't nice."

She readjusted her seat and looked ready to speak, as though stirred to answer a question that had lingered for many years. "Oh, you are taking me back to memories inscribed on the walls of al-Shawaka. Poor Salwa was one of the victims of Aliwi al-Attar. If you want to know her story, you should know what type of fox this man was who never had enough of women's bodies even though he had four wives. The fourth one refused to succumb to his desires. She was deaf and dumb.

"He used to claim that he was equally connected to angels and devils and attained his desires by using his knowledge of popular medicine. Sterile women, unmarried girls, and women left by their husbands used to resort to him. He was always ready to provide financial help, claiming to draw hearts closer to fearing God by chasing away the ghost of poverty and need. Aliwi al-Attar was pious in front of the people and always in the mosques, but no one knew his real intentions. He had a split personality, and people didn't want to believe that he was a beast under the surface. Rumor had it that he used to strip women of their clothes and massage their bodies with scented oils, claiming that he would deliver them from evil souls. Some women visited him for this purpose, either out of ignorance or out of feigned ignorance just to assuage their lust.

"How many times he chased me lasciviously I don't know—but he was unsuccessful. Before I turned forty, I was already a widow. My body was still fresh, and my skin was as soft as when I was in my twenties, but despite my wretched life I remained unaffected by him and resisted. I was a midwife, the only midwife in al-Shawaka. Most of that place's sons were born at my hands, among them three of Aliwi al-Attar's sons. Can you believe it? I used to pull a baby from his mother's womb without any problem, even during difficult births. But I left the profession after one of the women almost died at my hands because of her thinness and young age."

Mother Khadija had strayed from my question, but I didn't want to interrupt her.

"I warned the women about al-Attar's ruses and the traps he would set, so his desperation for me turned into hate. His grocery store was just in front of my house—I couldn't miss it. At that time, Salwa was only fifteen years old, soft and beautiful, her breasts getting round. She'd lost her mother; her father was taking care of her and her younger brother. One day she came to me and threw herself on my lap as though I were her mother; she was wailing as she said, 'If you don't help me, I will commit suicide.'

"Given my experience with women, I didn't need more explanation. I'd heard many similar stories.

"'How many months?'

"'Three.'

"'How did it happen?'

"She didn't answer, but I insisted and asked for the details before I could proceed with the abortion. She kissed my hands and cried. I assured her that many in similar circumstances had asked for my help and that her secret would be safe.

"Her brother Hassan had failed at school and feared his father's punishment, so he hid for three days. People were looking for him in neighboring places, among relatives, and in the hospitals. Her father had informed the police. Before sunset on the third day of his disappearance, as Salwa was making her way home from the search, Aliwi had met her on the street, claiming to know where Hassan was.

"'Where?' she had asked him, shaking as he put his hand on her shoulder.

"'At the haunted house.'

"She'd shivered, but Aliwi assured her with a confident voice, 'Don't worry, he's safe.'

"One house had been abandoned for years, and strange stories would circulate about it. Every time a family would live there, one of them would go mad or die at the new moon, until the house had turned into ruins, haunted by devils and ghosts."

Mother Khadija fell silent. She was tired, but I urged her to tell me the story of Salwa and Aliwi al-Attar.

"'We have to save Hassan before he loses his mind,' Salwa said.

"He was fingering his beads, mumbling, 'Wait for me here, in this corner.'

"He climbed the fence of the haunted house and asked her to come closer. She climbed the wall, and they found themselves in a yard filled with junk. As Salwa explained it to me, she hadn't been afraid. Like many, she had thought that al-Attar enjoyed a favored position with angels and devils. The two went inside, al-Attar first, then Salwa, leaning on his arm. They walked along a narrow corridor. Then he stopped her and asked her to keep silent.

"'Stay here.'

"He walked to the end of the corridor and disappeared behind one of the doors."

Mother Khadija interrupted her story to ask me if I wanted some tea or if I was hungry. "Let me know. Don't be shy. I'm like your mother. I have lentil soup and cooked cheese."

"Mother Khadija, I'm eager to know the rest of the story."

"Come every day, and you'll hear a more horrible story. I'm at the last station. Why should the stories die with me?"

"So what happened to Salwa after that?"

"She was agitated, both fearing the unknown and trusting at the same time. As she was torn between these feelings, Aliwi al-Attar appeared and asked her to come closer.

"Salwa then told me, 'I followed him, as he asked me, to the room he had just come out of. The floor was covered with a long carpet, on which there was a blanket and a woolen pillow, and there were magazine pictures of naked women on the walls. A few moments later he took me by surprise, out of breath like a bull. I couldn't run away or free myself from his arms.'

"It seemed that he had prepared the weapons of the hunt and chosen a prey that was unaware of his plans. The devil in him came out from under his clothes and raped her. I had to save her from the scandal. As for her brother Hassan, it turned out that he had taken refuge at a friend's place. After that incident, I didn't see Salwa for a while. Her family moved to the banking neighborhood, and six years passed before we met again in the Factory of Hope. She was upset to see me, perhaps because I was the only one who could remind her of that scandal. As for Aliwi al-Attar, he took his secrets to his tomb and died pierced by an uncountable number of knives. No one knew who had killed him, and none of his acquaintances was suspected of anything. The incident was reported as an unsolved case. From what I understood, a woman killed him to get rid of shame or to take revenge. The report also said that a police officer found a notebook where al-Attar had listed the names of all the women he had slept with, but because the police-man didn't want to see killings in every house, he tore it up."

THAT EVENING Samih was looking livelier. He slowly sipped his coffee while saying, "God has given us the best of senses, but most of the time we misuse them. Some people might live with good senses, but they don't come to enjoy life's pleasures, so their senses are beyond what they need. Some lose one of their senses and try to develop other senses. As for me, I see the world with what my fingers can play on its chords."

"Which sense is most vital?" I asked.

He answered, "All of them are vital, but I feel sorry for the dumb and deaf. The former can't speak, but he sees and hears; thus, he loses the pleasure of conversation. The latter is even more miserable because he can't hear the sounds of nature. Things around him seem like swimming in the void."

"It is a real problem; the most painful, though, is to lose the pleasure of life when one has his five senses."

He clapped happily with his hands, as if he just found something he had lost. "You begin to understand me.

That's why you should value what God gave you: you see, hear, and converse, taste, enjoy touching and smelling."

"You're right. I'm not enjoying life as I should. Exile plagues me, and the past has me almost in a stranglehold."

"In this case, either you reconcile with your memory, or you have to create a memory for the future."

"Perhaps memory's weight will lessen with time. But the creation of a new memory won't be very intimate because our most beautiful and important memories start when we are young and grow with us. They are shaped over the years by our family, childhood, and early friendships. And because they are virgin memories, they dig deep and suck the strength of the heart once in exile."

"One has to create one's happiness or at least feel contented wherever one finds oneself. That's how we can protect ourselves against erosion. Satisfaction is a blessing, and self-satisfaction is the highest degree of this blessing. If you would stop worrying, you would see that the world is opening its doors to you."

"It is possible to contain my personal worries, but what can I do with my country's sorrow? Its children are scattered, and its holy sites brutalized. Fifty years ago we fought against colonialism; now we begin to regret its passing because of our leaders' atrocities."

"Countries are bigger and live longer than their leaders. No matter how many destructive means a leader has, he cannot kill a homeland. You'll remember what I'm saying. The most important thing now is to treat your heart's wounds and open up to life. Live it without masks. Look for the beauty around you. I'm sure if I asked you about the color of your dress, you would not know. The seeing beings, except a few of them, have no visual culture. That's why they lose the meaning of beauty over the years."

"My circumstances are not too bad; I just find it difficult to adjust to them."

A small silence passed. I felt annoyed with myself because I always brought sadness whenever I sat with others. As I was about to excuse myself, Samih's fingers started hitting the strings of his lute, and my eyes shed bitter tears. The music flowed, washing my soul and freeing it of all fatigue. It was like a siren who had lived for ages at the bottom of the sea and then been thrown on a sandy beach. The playing continued harmoniously, a deaf instrument telling the most beautiful stories with fingers and feelings.

I hovered outside time and space, and I felt I was ten women in the body of one. The first woman fled along the road of the desert, the second wandered on the streets, the third was alone and lonely, the fourth whinnied like an indomitable horse, the fifth bid farewell to a man who forgot to tell her good-bye, the sixth strung her tears into a necklace for seasons of love that didn't come, the seventh hovered above the clouds, the eighth was patching up the defective garb of exile, the ninth witnessed her death and walked in her funeral procession, and the tenth was screaming at the final stroke in the performance, trying to remember an appointment that had passed more than a week ago.

I DIDN'T GET IN TOUCH WITH MOOSA—how long had it been since I last saw him?—but he was on my mind. I hadn't fallen in love with him, but I was dreaming about him as a man I could trust. As for the ambiguity in his eyes, I had just invented it. I told myself that women always look for someone to torture them, and if we don't find that person in others, he will spring up from under our skin. Women do not desire certainty; it's boring.

That evening I looked at things without ambiguity. My head was free of illusions, and I was opening up to welcome life. The change wasn't merely a mood shift; I knew it was time for me to settle. I would say yes to Moosa, and I would say it with complete certitude.

After a sleepless night, I found out that I was really leaning toward Moosa; my senses were awakening, waiting for his caress. I began to hear his voice—a fresh voice, whispering that life is an exhausting journey but that I have to live it fully.

The rain knocked on the door and played slowly on the window while I fell asleep. I would tell him that I had been double-checking with myself. He would not be angry with me; he loved me. We would be together. Sleep conquered me.

That night I ran on an endless carpet of grass and flowers crossed by streams and surrounded by fern and oleander trees. My steps were followed by music. I walked proudly to an unknown place that only my dreams' memory recognized. I walked while the streams murmured and colorful birds hovered with synchronized songs. The blue sky was embroidered with white clouds. A cart drawn by a golden horse came out of the diaphanous cloud. It halted near me, and from behind its velvety screens I could hear a voice calling me. Like a light bird, I jumped into the cart. The roaring wind pushed the cart mercilessly, and it flew far away. I screamed with all my force to the wind: "Stop your fury and cross the wide deserts! Take me back to Iraq's border or strike out these arid, infested times so that innocence may reveal itself!" The horse neighed and reared as if in danger, his coat turning from a transparent gold into a shining light. I rubbed my eyes and awoke exhausted, as though returning from a weary journey.

THE SUN'S RAYS showered on the buildings. The air was filled with the scent of flowers. The streets were clean, and the morning just beginning. I prepared my words. It had been a month now. I would tell him that my feelings had been mixed. He knew that. Before I left for the telephone booth, I put my camel-bone necklace around my neck. I dialed the number.

"Yes?"

"Sorry, I think I have the wrong number."

I dialed the number again, and the same voice answered.

"Yes, who is this?"

"I'm sorry. I'd like to speak to Moosa."

"Moosa left. He went to Australia five days ago. I'm his friend Faisal."

A bitter silence passed. He interrupted it, asking, "Are you Huda?"

"Yes, I'm Huda."

"He asked me to take care of you. If you need anything, call me. Think of me as your brother."

"Thank you."

"Moosa called yesterday. Once he's settled, he'll send his address. Do you have a phone number?"

"No, I'll contact you. Thank you."

At the first sign of spring, Moosa had left for Australia. We hadn't bid each other farewell, and I didn't have any explanation for what happened. I was bitter. Painful words took over and began to whip me. The other woman inside me awoke and began oppressing me.

"The opportunity was there, Huda. It knocked at your door more than once, but you were preoccupied, busy. You spent your days asking sterile questions, falling into the well of memories, and distorting the present. Everything else changed taste and color except you. You looked at Moosa's feelings as though you controlled destinies. He was bored with your mood changes and your agitated feelings. He departed without a word of farewell, leaving you with a store of memories. Don't say you loved him. You were always looking for a love that didn't exist. You are a swaying soul. You have the same mood fluctuations as the river that witnessed your birth, and you will never enjoy the taste of love. Train yourself from now on to erase your wounds and keep the memories, but be careful not to get hurt."

I found myself in my cold room, my teeth chattering. From afar, I could hear a cat's mewing, asking for help. While I was moaning under the blankets, trying to restrain my feelings, I said to myself, "You have nothing to lose in exile; you already lost everything when you left."

The other woman attacked back, shaking me. "You are a scattered woman, difficult to put together."

I said to her, "But I carry in me feelings of love that I'm sure one day will overflow."

She yelled at me, "Stop it!"

The mewing of the cat outside the door became inaudible, and my body relaxed, but my head was crowded with tens of faces wearing Moosa's features.

THERE WAS A VASE with artificial flowers on a rectangular table. Three persons were seated at this table: the translator, the American delegate, and I. I looked at the American: a sharp face with piercing blue eyes. I tried to find in them something that would assuage my anxiety.

I was shaking. The American's questions came at me through the translator.

They were mostly the same questions that I had answered in my first meeting with the relocation official. The American delegate wanted to be sure about what I had said. I answered carefully and didn't lie, didn't falsify any claim.

After about twenty minutes, the meeting was over. The translator informed me that my relocation in America depended on the delegate and that they would be in touch soon.

"Congratulations."

I heard that comment from many people as I walked out, but I left the office without responding. Something inside was squeezing me. I said to myself, "I should have changed my answers; perhaps the American delegate will reject me."

Scared, I walked to the bus stop. I was so perplexed I almost crossed the street without noticing the traffic light. I was absentminded and not focusing on anything. Truncated images of faces and stories from different times got mixed up with the noise of the cars and the clamor of the street.

I went into my room and closed the door carefully. I was afraid. I tried to rid myself of the idea that something was following me. I took off my clothes (sweaty in spite of the cold air) and slipped into my bed. The American delegate's face with its blue eyes jumped out at me. He kept asking me the same questions, and I kept giving the same answers, but distorting them a little bit by changing the dates. He was looking at me distrustfully, so I implored him, "Please—I'm not good for America."

His face sharpened, and he didn't say a word. I was the one talking. I raved, I prattled, I turned the answers upside down. He held his head, clenched his fist, and hit the table, yelling, "You are rejected!"

AMERICA DIDN'T REJECT ME. When I received the Refugee Office's answer a week later, I just said, "Thank you." My feelings were neutral. I wasn't happy, but at the same time I didn't plunge into sadness. I said to myself again, "I have nothing to lose; I've already lost a lot. Perhaps it is only politics that has depicted America as a monster devouring the world."

Contrary to my previous habits, I wasn't exaggerating my fantasies about how horrible things might turn out. I was following the invisible stream that determines the steps and draws the itineraries of our lives. I was able to remove my mask in Amman's streets and walk naturally, without asking myself so many questions. Even my grandmother's voice had ceased to repeat her warnings to me. Youssef was becoming just part of the past. And Moosa, I found out through him that I had only liked the idea of being in love, as if I had wanted to avoid falling into the void.

WHILE I WAS HAVING COFFEE, Samih said, "You'll be off for a few days."

"What do you mean?"

"The Ministry of Culture has chosen five lute players, including myself, to participate in a festival in Cairo. It's the first time I will travel outside Jordan."

"I'll miss you. I will really miss you. I've gotten used to these feelings, poetry, music, and conversation."

"I won't stay too long. But you should prepare yourself for an intensive schedule before I go. I would like to listen to more of al-Sayyab's poems. This poet awakens in me deep feelings that I can express only with music. I have in mind a project about al-Sayyab's exile. For that I'll need your help."

"I'll help you. I'm sure this project will be an important transition in your artistic career."

"In addition to what we have here in the library, Samiha can provide you with books about al-Sayyab."

He seemed about to say something, but he kept silent, so I asked, "Is there anything you want to say?"

"I wish you could take off the mask that keeps you from seeing the truth."

I didn't understand and was confused, but I said, "Sometimes we need masks to protect ourselves. That doesn't mean that we don't see the truth."

"Sometimes, but not always."

"Our emotional state is what determines truth. If I'm down, do I want the whole world to know about it?"

"Only if the mask doesn't become the rule."

"I promise many things in me will change."

"Get ready for the new experience awaiting you in America."

"I look forward to it."

I DIDN'T VISIT MOTHER KHADIJA AGAIN and would never know what happened to her.

One day I found myself in the Hashemite Square, where she usually sat with Umm Hashim. They weren't there. I walked downtown, looking at tired Iraqi faces. Near Restaurant al-Quds, I saw Umm Hashim; she was putting her money in her wallet. I picked up some incense sticks and gave her money. She didn't look at me.

"How are you, Umm Hashim?" I asked.

As soon as she lifted her eyes, she began imploring me to take back the quarter of a pound.

"No need to be generous, Umm Hashim. Tell me, where is Mother Khadija?"

"Oh, she left a while ago. As soon as she felt better, she decided to go back to Iraq. She said she wanted to die there, although she has no children. But she left a message for you."

"What message?"

"She said, 'Don't ever travel to America.'"

"And what do you think?"

"Frankly, my daughter, I have another opinion."

"What is it?"

"Anyplace in the world is fine for us as long as we can live with dignity. Our life has become bitter. Go wherever you go, and God protect you."

DATES DON'T MEAN ANYTHING when they don't leave a mark in the memory. Throughout the journey of our lives, some dates get inscribed, and others are erased. The dates that remain are those of birth, death, the first shiver of love, big joys and deep sadness, the last glance before departure, the last waves, and tears of farewells. Some dates are like pins poking the skin, producing the nervous prickling of fear. Some engrave themselves in the footsteps, on the walls, and in the heartbeat, whereas others spring up to hammer the head again and again during life's journey.

March 4 will remain engraved as the birth of my new life. It's the day I would be leaving Amman for America. Here I was packing up my life into a bundle of thrift-shop clothing smelling of mothballs. I would also take a few Arabic books that I would need there, before I learned the new language. One bag would be enough; I would be getting rid of many things. I didn't get the time to participate in Samih's project. He called Samiha yesterday and said that he would be late. I sorted my papers—pages onto which I had transcribed my pain, papers with addresses and unimportant notes. I wouldn't need Nadia's diary. I didn't wish to carry sorrows, but my hand wouldn't let me tear it up. I would leave it there, on the table or under the bed, or perhaps I would bury it so that it would live longer, under the grape-seed tree. I wouldn't need her small bag with her personal belongings. I hadn't opened it when I picked up her things, so I opened it that day: eyeliner, a notebook, and a leather wallet. A photo of Nadia was in one of its pockets, a gloomy photo of a sad woman. I couldn't look at it long, lest I fell into a fit of crying. But as soon as I examined the other pocket, I almost fainted from the surprise. My body tingled, my joints weakened, and my fingers went numb. A cry was stifled in my chest.

In the other pocket was a photo of Moosa. I could see it clearly; I wasn't dreaming. It was Moosa, although he looked a few years younger. I looked at the photo—it read "Your Emir." I remembered the letters that she began repeatedly with "My Emir." I could hear his voice saying, "I fled with my brother's identity. I wanted to preserve his memory. That's why I kept his name." I hadn't thought then to ask him about his real name.

My body was still absorbing the effect of the surprise. After a few minutes, I rushed to the phone booth and called Faisal. I wrote down Moosa's address.

Don't worry, Nadia, your letters will reach him. I sent the diary in an envelope without my name on it. I just wrote on a small piece of paper, "Nadia died, and this is what she left for you."

That night Nadia came to me in my dreams. She wasn't angry or annoyed. Her face shone, and her soul was settled. She waved at me and disappeared.

Fate had been kind to Moosa; they didn't meet again. How would his days have been if he had had to take her to the grave after this great love? Time had played its game with them. One after the other, each of them had come to Amman but had never met. After such a separation, though, her letters would still find him. I wondered how he would receive their abundance of impassioned feelings.

I didn't ask myself whether what I did was the right thing to do, but I did wonder what would have happened if I had found out about Moosa after I married him.

I would have fallen into endless sadness if not for an instant in which I felt that I was no longer the same person. I was no longer an easy prey to sorrow, and memories couldn't scare me. Another face, perhaps a new mask, was on me. Nadia's letters had inflamed me; they made me seek refuge in Moosa and escape my bitter memories, but without any consideration of my real feelings.

I brushed off my hands and began putting my things in order. March 4 would separate the two stages of my life. On that day I could begin looking at Amman's streets with affection, paying attention to their details, filling my chest with the city's air. I could feel the market's crowd— the same crowd I used to avoid. Strangely enough, I didn't grow nostalgic. Where was this strong sense of resolution coming from? Only eight days before I traveled.

After Samih heard about my travel plans, he called from Cairo to talk to me. He wished me happiness, but behind his voice I could feel suppressed weeping. The time for departure was approaching. One after another, I crossed out each day on the calendar.

Only four days were left. I had gotten rid of surplus possessions, and everything was ready for the journey. Samih hadn't returned from Cairo. Samiha told me that he had met the Iraqi musician Nasseer Shamma, who asked him to join his group (the House of Arab Lute), and he was considering the offer. One day after another. The hands of the clock were running. Only two days left.

I was not happy or sad, satisfied or angry. I wanted to discover the unknown and felt like a newborn. It was my last day in Amman—Amman that was bringing me my country's news through the waves of immigrants who were looking for their bread and escaping the fires of new wars. The exile I had suffered would be a mere rehearsal for longer days that would begin tomorrow.

IT'S MARCH 4. Samiha helps me carry my bag. She puts it in her car, and while she takes me to Queen Alya Airport, my eyes gather details of Amman before I miss it forever. A voice behind me cries: "Oh, stranger, where to?" And

I repeat to myself what the poet Ibrahim al-Zabidi said when he departed for freedom thirty years ago:

Oh, morning of Baghdad, Farewell,
I'm entering exile.